Desperate Horse Wives

Janet R Fox

To Ann,

Happy trails to you! May we camp together again. Try the eggs-in-a-basket. Happy reading. Janet R Joy

DEDICATION

To Jack, my knight in shining armor,

And to my brother, Dave, who is greatly missed and still loved by so many,

And to the many volunteers who create and maintain Ohio horse trails.

CONTENTS

CHAPTER 1
DESPERATE HORSE WIVES

It was a Friday night in mid-May.

Nancy pushed herself from her lawn chair and tossed another log on the campfire. She used a long stick to move the burning logs around until the flames danced a little higher. She smiled at the group of women sitting around the fire in the near dark. They were in the horseman's camp at Beaver Creek State Park in Ohio, near the Pennsylvania border.

These women were Nancy's collection of friends, each one found while she was shopping at Walmart. Priceless.

At sixty-nine, Nancy was often the first one to leave the group for her trailer to go to bed. She brushed her fingers through her graying hair and slid her glasses back in place on her nose. "I'm going to check my horse and turn in. Since we want to ride early tomorrow before the afternoon heat, how about breakfast at seven-thirty?"

The other women, mesmerized by the fire, murmured their agreement for an early start.

Nancy walked the short distance to her gooseneck horse trailer. Like the ones belonging to the other three women, it had living quarters in front with three horse stalls in the rear. Nancy had just one horse, but she used the second stall for hay and grain, and the third stall for camping gear like the wheelbarrow and lawn chair. The saddle, bridle, and other tack hung in the tack room in back next to the ramp where the horse entered. A barrel with water for the horse lay in the bed of the three-quarter ton pickup truck.

"Hello, Bright Beauty. How are you doing?" Nancy rubbed the velvety nose of her golden palomino Missouri Fox Trotter mare picketed on the high line the park had strung between two posts. These picket lines were installed around the whole perimeter of the horseman's camp. Campers tied their horses to these lines with a lead rope clipped to a halter when they were not riding on the bridle trails. They hung bales of hay from the lines so that the horses could eat as often as they wanted. The lines were high so that the horses could move under them, but not put their legs across them, or tangle a leg in the lead rope, and hurt themselves.

"You ate most of your hay already. This won't last the rest of the night." Nancy pulled a fresh bale from the trailer and pulled and tugged it into a hay bag made of rope netting. She climbed on her step stool and replaced the nearly empty hay bag hanging from the line with the full one. She topped off the water in Beauty's bucket, gave her a gentle rub on her neck and turned in for the night. She was grateful for the self-contained living quarters with three-burner stove, refrigerator, double sink, couch, queen-size bed, and bathroom complete with shower. Even if it rained, Nancy and the others were comfortable on a camping trip.

At the campfire, Elise looked at Lavern. "How are you doing with Charlie? Is he any less controlling since you've been going to counseling?"

Lavern, the youngest adult in the group at twenty-four, frowned. "No, actually the counselor told me that people who need to control others rarely change. She said that if I love him enough, and if I feel safe, I'll probably just have to endure his controlling ways. Men like him often become abusive. So far, he just controls verbally. The counselor said that his need to control me could stem from jealousy. We've only been married for two years. Maybe in time he'll learn to trust me." Lavern's pretty mouth still frowned.

"No, he never will. The counselor's right. He won't change. You need to get out," Bristol advised her.

"In the meantime, he's insisting that we have a baby. I mean, he knows I really don't want to start a family now. I can't explain why to him, but I feel that he wouldn't be a good father. I think that he doesn't really want a baby so much as he wants to tie me down to the house so I can't do things like coming on these horse camping trips with you girls. No, I don't think he would be a good father, so I don't want to have children with him. Maybe I don't even want him at all. I just don't know." Lavern brushed a tear from the corner of her eye.

Elise reached out to her and squeezed her hand. "I'm sorry, Honey. I'm really glad, though, that you have the strength to come on these weekend trips in spite of his objections. Geez, we only do this six times a year." The women came on monthly horse campouts May through October.

Elise continued, "It's too bad that he can't learn that giving you some independence can make you appreciate him more, and that trying to tie you down can be the downfall of the relationship."

"Right. He kind of forces me to be someone I don't like so well. Like now I'm secretly taking birth control pills. I hate to be sneaky. And I hate our fights about me coming riding. Yet he refuses to come riding with me. We could afford another horse. He wants me to sell Lacy and go on road trips with him on his motorcycle all summer. Oh, well, at least I ride Lacy in spite of him. I guess I have to count my blessings."

Elise hoped that her sixteen-year-old daughter Jolene would fall in love with a man who would treat her with respect. Her husband, Marty, was not a good role model for Jolene in that area. He tended to spoil Jolene and allow her too much freedom, and he was disrespectful to Elise sometimes. Now that Jolene was a teen, she was also showing signs of disrespect to her mother. Elise felt that Marty should stand up for her, but he ignored the little verbal jabs Jolene gave her while sometimes adding sarcastic remarks of his own.

"Yes, Lavern," Elise agreed. "We do have many blessings to count. It's easier for me to do that out here in the woods and while riding my horse down the trail. It tends to put my life into better perspective."

"Yup. I know what you mean. I need these fixes to keep my spirits up. I also need a good night's sleep. See you in the morning." Lavern stood, folded her chair, and walked off to tend her horse, and then go to bed.

Bristol, as short as Nancy but two years younger and sixty pounds heavier, muttered something derogatory under her breath about Lavern not being any fun anymore. No one paid any attention to her. The others were used to her nasty comments, no one agreed with them, and each figured that Bristol was sick in some way. Bristol Monarch, living up to her name, behaved as though she thought she were royalty. Her husband, Richard, was a prince of a man, although Bristol did not speak of him that way. They tolerated her because Nancy had befriended Bristol before any of them, and so they had to put up with Bristol belonging to the group.

Bristol stood, slammed her lawn chair closed, and marched off to check her horse without saying anything more.

"She must be going to bed, too," Elise said in a neutral tone. She hoped so. She wanted to enjoy the fire in peace. Jolene was stretched in a lounge chair, eyes closed, long blond hair spread around her head, either asleep or very relaxed. Elise wondered how her daughter was so beautiful. Elise herself had an unremarkable face and plain, short, brown hair that never held a style. Her husband, Marty, was your average nice-looking man, but not really handsome. Jolene was truly fortunate to be tall and slender with a pretty face and beautiful hair.

A peaceful hour later, Elise kicked apart the few logs on the fire and determined that the coals would burn down safely. She folded her chair and gently shook Jolene's arm.

"What?" Jolene whined.

"Honey, don't you want to go to bed to sleep? It's late and no one else is by the fire now."

"Yeah, yeah, OK. In a minute."

"Go ahead and get up. I'll check on our horses. I'll see you inside. Fold up your chair and put it away so the dew won't get it wet."

"I will," Jolene said, irritated to be told to do something she would have done anyway.

Elise checked on the hay and water for Tricked Out and Tucker, their black Tennessee Walker geldings. Trick had a white blaze, white stockings to his knees, and a large white spot on his shoulder. Tucker had a white blaze and one white sock. She gave a tug on each lead rope to be sure that they were tight enough to keep the horses on the picket line. If a horse came loose, it would stay fairly near the other horses, but the tied horses would cause a commotion whinnying, which would wake the campers. Elise did not want the embarrassment of being a dude, someone without horsemanship skills.

The stars were bright in the cloudless sky. The evening air was cool but comfortable. The horses all along the line were quietly resting or sleeping. Lavern's Tennessee Walker mare, Lacy, was lying down, feet tucked under, head up and resting against the pull of the lead rope. No one else stirred in horse camp.

****

The morning dawned at six o'clock. The birds were chirping, the horses were stirring, and the dew was still on the ground. Nancy was already feeding Bright Beauty her morning grain ration. Beauty was knocking the grain bucket about, swinging it on the rope that hung it from the picket line. The other horses nickered and whinnied asking for their grain. Nancy mucked the manure from under Beauty's feet, piled it in the wheelbarrow, and rolled it to the dumping site.

Lavern was up next. She tended to her mare, Lacy, a rich brown chestnut, with black mane, tail, and stockings.

Elise came out of her trailer with three cups of coffee on a tray. She offered a cup to Nancy and to Lavern. "How can you girls work this early before coffee? I have to wake up first." She pulled out her chair and sat down to enjoy the hot brew. She pulled her denim jacket closed over her purple tee shirt in the cool morning air. All of the women wore blue jeans and tee shirts.

Nancy finished with her horse, picked up her coffee, and pulled her chair next to Elise's under the awning attached to Bristol's trailer. The group parked their rigs with Nancy and

Bristol's trailers facing each other, the two awnings nearly touching. Behind them, Elise's and Lavern's rigs were parked facing each other.

Just after Lavern brought her chair around to enjoy the first cup of morning coffee with the others, Bristol opened her trailer door. Ignoring the other two, she looked at Elise and said, "Why are you drinking coffee instead of taking care of your horse? Some people are so selfish taking care of themselves before their horses. I bet you didn't bring me any coffee either, did you?"

Before Elise could answer, Bristol slammed her door.

"Maybe she went back to bed," Nancy said between sips of coffee.

"I hope so," Lavern answered. "She needs to get up again from the other side."

"I'm no more selfish to drink my coffee first before taking care of my two horses than she is for sleeping in instead of tending to hers." Elise was angry.

"Shh," Nancy warned them, pointing to Bristol's camper. "Don't make it worse."

"Hey, let's get the water boiling for our eggs-in-a-bag breakfast. That will take awhile. I'll feed, water, and muck after we have it set up." Elise was determined not to immediately tend her horses just to spite Bristol a little.

The women set up a folding table under Elise's awning, by unspoken agreement moving farther from Bristol's trailer. Nancy brought out her Coleman stove. They set water to boil in a large pot. They began to set up for breakfast with a tablecloth, paper plates, napkins, and plastic ware. They had paper cups for juice, but everyone used ceramic mugs for their coffee. They set out a dozen eggs, chopped green peppers, chopped onions, and grated yellow cheese. Lavern went to her trailer to fry bacon, and Elise went to tend her horses.

By seven-thirty, the horses were tended and the water was boiling. A pitcher of orange juice and a pot of coffee were placed with the other food on the table. Elise had called Jolene to wake her up, but Bristol had not made another appearance. The early risers sat under Elise's awning happily chatting.

"How long should we wait for Bristol?" Lavern asked.

"Maybe until eight o'clock," Nancy answered. "We really need to eat so we can ride."

"Yeah, I'm hungry," Elise said. "All that mucking manure makes you hungry." She looked at Jolene, hoping that Jolene would thank her for tending to her horse. Jolene was busy checking her cell phone for text messages.

At eight o'clock, the women gave up on Bristol and began filling their individual plastic freezer bags with eggs, and with any combination of the green peppers, onions, cheese and bacon. They mashed them up together and sealed the bags closed before placing them in the boiling water for their eggs-in-a-bag breakfast. When they finished eating, they left the dishes of food on the table and the boiling water on the stove for Bristol. Nancy knocked on Bristol's trailer door and told her she needed to get up if she intended on riding with them. "Come on out and eat your breakfast."

Nancy, Lavern, Elise, and Jolene led their horses from the picket line to the opposite side of their trailers from their awnings, and began to groom the horses before saddling them. A few minutes later, Bristol appeared to feed her black and white Spotted Saddle Horse gelding, Hot Stuff. When he finished his grain,

Bristol led him to her trailer to groom and saddle for the ride. Nancy walked over and asked her if she was going to eat her eggs-in-a-bag.

"No, I ate an apple and a breakfast bar this morning." Bristol continued to brush her horse.

"Well," Nancy told her, "next time let us know. We didn't have the mushrooms or the red peppers or the grapefruit juice you were going to contribute, and we waited for you for half an hour, and then we left all the food on the table for you."

"I didn't want eggs this morning," she snapped.

Nancy suspected that Bristol didn't want the company of the women, either, but it was still rude of her not to let them know that she would not be joining them. Also, she could have given them her contributions to the breakfast. Nancy put away all the paper products. She placed plastic wrap over all the food dishes and stuck hers in her refrigerator. She told the others that they could pick up their food items, saying only that Bristol was finished with them.

The women were saddling their horses. Each of them rode with a breast collar to keep the saddle from slipping back and a crupper to keep the saddle from slipping forward. They clipped lead ropes to the D rings so they could tie their horses on the trail, and they hung water bottles in holders from the saddles. They packed a lunch in either a cantle bag for the rear of the saddle or a pommel bag for the front of the saddle. No one tied on a raincoat this morning. They each had a helmet for safety.

Jolene was fussing at her mother, refusing to wear her helmet. "Mom," she said, drawing the word into two syllables, "It's hot and it looks weird."

"You know the rule. You wear that helmet if you're going to ride. Otherwise, you don't go. I'm tired of this argument with you every time we're about to ride. After you wear it for a few minutes, you don't notice it's there. You don't look weird, either. You look smart. It's stupid not to protect your head. Just feel lucky I don't also have you in a protective vest for your ribs. They *are* hot."

"Come on, Mom. We can trust Trick. She's safe."

"Right, she is a pretty safe horse," Elise agreed, "but she's still an animal with her own mind. Maybe her name is Trick for Tricky. Besides, we don't know what might happen on the trail."

"Mom," two syllables again, "you know her name is Tricked Out." Jolene did not appreciate Elise's attempt at humor.

"Tell me now. Either you wear the helmet and we both go riding, or you don't wear it and we both stay in camp."

In answer, Jolene shoved the helmet on her head and swung onto Tricked Out's back. The walking horse pranced in anticipation as the others mounted their horses. All their horses were easy-gaited breeds with a smooth four-beat gait instead of a three-beat trot. The women had purchased their horses for easy riding because they rode trails for three, four, and sometimes five hours at a time. The horses covered more ground at a flat-footed walk than trotting horses, and when moved up into their specialty gaits, they seemed to float.

"Do you still want to follow the longer orange trail today and go to the main park for our lunch break?" Nancy asked the group.

"Yes! I want to cross the river. It should be like really fun after all the rain we had this week," Jolene said.

"Lead on," Lavern answered. "Let's go!"

"If the river's too swift at the crossing, we'll be turning around," Elise told the women. Nancy and Lavern agreed. Jolene did not want to turn around, but she decided not to argue at this point. Maybe she would not have to.

Jolene placed Trick in the front of the group. Elise was right behind her on Tucker who did not want his barn buddy Trick to be far from him. Next came Lavern on Lacy followed by Nancy on Bright Beauty. Bristol, on Hot Stuff, found herself in the rear. They rode their horses out of camp, across the road, and through the meadow. Although the temperature was expected to rise into the mid 90's, at nine-fifteen in the morning it was still cool enough to be comfortable. After a left turn, the trail turned into the woods and went down a long hill. At the bottom, the trail turned right and crossed a stone-filled creek before winding uphill again. The area was rocky, hilly, wooded, green, and beautiful. The fresh air smelled of damp earth. The riders were relaxed and happy as they enjoyed the scenery, their horses, and their companionship.

After following the orange trail for nearly two hours, they reached the river. On the other side was the main park where there were picket lines, picnic tables, and restrooms. It was a perfect place to take a lunch break. The riders lined up at the crossing. The water was high and swift, very dark, and maybe three feet deep. Even Jolene had second thoughts about crossing until Bristol pushed past her on Hot Stuff, causing Tricked Out to move over a step. Hot Stuff brushed against Jolene's knee as Bristol challenged, "Come on you dudes. You can do this."

Hot Stuff hesitated to enter the river, so Bristol jabbed him once with her spurs. He entered the water. One by one, the other horses followed.

Nancy called a warning to the others. "Don't look down at the water. You'll get dizzy. Look across to the shore."

"Slow Trick down," Elise yelled to Jolene. "These rocks are slippery, and the current's strong."

Jolene slowed her horse so he could carefully place one hoof at a time across the rocks. As they reached the center of the swollen river, Trick slipped and fell sideways, throwing Jolene out of the saddle on the downstream side. After hitting her head on a rock, the current carried her away from under the horse, a split second before Trick landed on his side, saving her from being crushed. Her flailing hands grabbed the stirrup, keeping her from floating down the river. Holding tight to the stirrup with her left hand, she reached higher with her right hand to grab the saddle horn and lift herself higher from the water. Trick struggled to stand against the current. Jolene lost her grip on the saddle horn, but grabbed the stirrup so that she again gripped it with both hands. Her feet floated straight behind her as she retained her panicked hold on the stirrup.

Elise watched in horrified shock as her daughter floated in the swift river while hanging on as Trick struggled to his feet. When he finally gained his feet, he stood, trembling. Jolene pulled herself up to a standing position on the moss-covered rocks. One foot after the other slipped from the rocks as she struggled to keep her balance and stay upright in the rushing water.

Elise pulled herself together and carefully rode Tucker to the downstream side of Jolene, who was unable to walk on the slippery rocks. In a shaky voice she said, "Here, Honey, grab my stirrup with your left hand and keep your hold on your stirrup with your right hand. We can get you to shore walking between the two horses."

Jolene used the two horses to steady herself. Now it was going to be difficult to walk the horses out slowly, side by side, keeping Jolene safe between them while she held onto the two stirrups. Elise had managed to reach for Trick's reins and now she worked to keep both horses at a slow pace, side by side, as Jolene struggled between them.

The current tried to take Jolene's legs downstream, pressing her against her mother's horse. She managed to remain upright and take one slow step at a time, but her feet kept slipping on the mossy rocks. If not for hanging onto the two stirrups she would have been down again. Her arms and shoulders ached with the effort of holding up her body as they slowly and carefully crossed the swift river.

Bristol, Lavern, and Nancy reached the far shore and turned their horses so they could see the progress the other two were making. Finally Elise and Jolene reached the shoreline. Elise stopped Tucker in the water and told Jolene to climb out with Trick. When Jolene was safe on dry land, Elise rode Tucker up the embankment and onto the shore, joining the women who were looking at Jolene's helmet. It was crushed on one side from her fall on the rocks.

"Mom, I'm sorry," Jolene told her while rubbing her shoulders and arms. "That could have been my skull. I'll never ride without it again."

Elise, weak with relief, slipped from her saddle, dropped to the ground and folded on her shaky knees. She began to cry.

"Oh, get over it," Bristol told her. "Jolene's all right. Put on your big girl panties and get back on your horse." Without waiting for Elise or Jolene to remount, Bristol turned her horse and headed down the trail.

"Oh, Honey, you scared me silly," Elise sobbed. "Thank goodness this trail is a loop, and we don't have to cross the river here again today." Elise stood and tried to mount Tucker, but her legs were too weak, and Tucker did not want to stand still. He wanted to follow Hot Stuff down the trail. Jolene gave her mother a boost into the saddle, then mounted Trick.

The women rode the short distance to the park through a row of pine trees, and dismounted by the picket lines. They dropped the bits from their trail bridles, turning them into halters. They tied their horses to the picket line with their lead ropes and unpacked their lunches. They put their lunches down on the picnic table where Bristol already sat, and headed for the restroom. Jolene peeled off her wet tee shirt and replaced it with her mother's denim jacket. Her jeans were wet, but not too uncomfortable in the rising temperature. She poured water out of her riding shoes, took her socks off, and put her wet shoes back on her feet.

They rejoined Bristol at the picnic table. Jolene was too revved up from adrenaline to eat. She kept talking about how it felt to be nearly carried downstream and how impressed she was that her helmet had saved her head. When she wore out that subject, she jabbered on about whatever came to her mind. She could not shut herself up.

Elise was also too upset to eat, but she was silent. She had been terrified to see her daughter in the cold, swift river.

Six other riders came to the picnic area and sat at a table next to theirs. Jolene told them about her experience and showed them her helmet.

"We figured the river would be too swift today, so we rode the trail here from the other direction," a man dressed in a cowboy shirt and jeans told her. "We'll go back the same way. Maybe we can cross in a couple of days."

"Well, we're only here for the weekend, so we won't be crossing it again this time," Bristol said, leaning toward him with her arms squeezing the maximum cleavage into the deep V neck of her tee shirt. "We came into camp yesterday afternoon. We rode a little on the blue trail. We'll do the rest of the orange loop today and hit the yellow trail tomorrow, then that's it for this weekend. Do you come here often?"

The man said that they did, and he introduced himself and the people with him. Nancy was glad that it turned out he was married to one of the ladies in his group since Bristol was also married. Her husband, Richard, or Ric, was a very nice man with more patience than Job from the Bible. He had to be patient to put up with Bristol's cutting remarks.

"Come on," Nancy told her group. "Let's hit the trail."

They threw their trash in the receptacle, gathered their lunch boxes and water bottles, and put their helmets back on their heads. Jolene and Elise fed the apples they did not eat to their mounts. Everyone packed their lunch boxes and water bottles onto their saddles. They put the bits back in their horses' mouths, untied their horses, rolled up the lead ropes and attached them back on their saddles.

"Riders up," Nancy said. "Let's go."

The group moved along through the grove of pine trees to the base of a long hill. To the left, the trail would take them back to the river crossing. They rode right. It was a long, rocky climb out of the valley to the top of a ridge. It was amazing how much hotter it was at the top. They traveled the trail along the ridge. Insects chirped, birds sang, and chipmunks and squirrels rustled through the brush. Through the trees was a view of the winding river in the valley far below. Finally the trail dropped to the valley floor again, and followed along the river. There were several more river crossings as the trail wound back and forth from one side of the water to the other. Although the water was deeper than normal, it was not as swift on this section of the ride.

After one more, long, rocky climb, they reached the horse camp on top. The horses were tired and sweaty, and so were the riders. Everyone untacked the horses at the trailers, filled buckets with water, and sponged off the animals. When the horses were cooled off, they were put back on the picket lines with fresh hay and water. Nancy, Elise, and Jolene retired to their trailers to take a nap. Bristol and Lavern sat under Lavern's awning.

"So, it's not going so well with your controlling husband, huh?" Bristol asked Lavern. "I think you should leave him. Then you can do whatever you want whenever you want."

"It isn't that simple," Lavern told her. "There's a lot of emotion and caring here as well as considerations like finances. I would rather he learn to stop trying to control me. I really do love him. I just don't like how he treats me sometimes."

A motorcycle came puttering down the camp road. Lavern's jaw tightened. She hoped that it wouldn't be her husband Charlie. It would be like him to come here just to check up on her.

"Hey, speak of the devil! Isn't that Charlie?" Bristol pointed. "Doesn't he ride a red Honda?"

"Yeah, that's him." Lavern stood up and waved in the direction of the road. Charlie nodded and rode the bike onto the grass and parked it near the trailer. He took off his helmet and ran his fingers through his long dark brown hair.

"Hello, ladies. Am I missing anything?"

"Like what would you be missing, Charlie?" Bristol asked him sarcastically.

"How about lunch? Did you eat?" Lavern grabbed another lawn chair and motioned for Charlie to sit down. He remained standing.

"Yeah, I ate before I rode down here. So what's up?"

"The sky," Bristol told him.

Lavern wished Bristol would leave, so she and Charlie could have a little privacy. If Charlie was angry or upset, Bristol could make it worse.

Lavern told Charlie that they had just returned from the ride. She told him about the river crossing and Jolene's spill into the water.

"Well, now, you see, that's just another good reason for you not to be doing this. This is dangerous. You not only could hurt yourself, but what if you were pregnant? You could lose the baby. Why don't you pack it up and follow me home? I'll even ride real slow for you."

"You talk about dangerous to Lavern when you ride that motorcycle? Aren't you using a double standard?" Bristol was incensed. No one was going to push her around, and she did not like to see other women being controlled by a man. Actually, Bristol did not think much of men in general.

Charlie turned his back on Bristol. "Come on Lavern. Let's go inside and talk." He took Lavern's hand and pulled her up from her chair. They went into the trailer.

Bristol could not understand why Lavern did not stand up for herself more. She tried to hear the conversation, but they were apparently talking too quietly. She gave up trying, and took her chair around to her trailer across from Nancy's. She sat under her awning, but no one else was around, and the flies were biting, so

24

she decided to go inside to take a nap.

****

The supper was planned for everyone to bring their own meat for the grill and a dish to share. Since there were two of them, Elise had brought a tossed salad with three kinds of dressing plus a plate of home-baked chocolate chip cookies. Nancy brought homemade baked beans, and Lavern contributed made-from-scratch potato salad. Bristol contributed a bowl of strawberries from the store. It was just the women for the meal. Charlie had left camp to ride his bike back home.

After dinner, Jolene set a fire inside the circle of stones ready to light at dusk. She checked her cell phone for text messages, and texted some of her friends. The others took care of their horses, feeding them grain, making sure they had hay and water, and mucking the manure from under their picket lines.

When it was nearly dark, the group gathered at the fire circle with their chairs.

"Where's Bristol?" Nancy asked, settling her chair away from the curling smoke.

"Oh, she's talking to some guy camped two sites up from us," Lavern told her. "Here, I brought the makings for S'mores." She handed out chocolate, marshmallows, and graham crackers. "Jolene, you have a good fire going. When it has some glowing coals, you can roast my marshmallows for me. I don't want mine burned."

Elise swatted at a mosquito. "Maybe we should sit in the smoke! Pesky things. Anyone want some of this mosquito spray?" She handed the can around.

"Nancy, how's your mother doing? Alzheimer's is a terrible disease. I know you are worn out and really need these trips to relax." Lavern was concerned for her friend who was trying to care for her mother without much help from a sister who lived out of town.

"Thanks for asking. We still have her in her own home, but we're fixing up our third bedroom for her in our house. It will probably be ready for her early next week. Harry's going to be painting in there this weekend since my sister is taking care of Mom so I can be here. Mom really shouldn't be alone anymore. Her neighbor watches over her a couple hours a day, but it isn't enough. We're afraid she'll start a fire or something, so even when she moves in with us, one of us will have to be there with her all the time. I wish my sister lived closer to help more." Nancy put a marshmallow on the end of a sharpened stick and placed it strategically in the fire so that it would burn to a black crisp. "At least Sis stays with Mom so I can come on our weekend rides."

Elise hoped Jolene would be there for her in her old age. Elise tried to encourage Nancy. "At least when your mother moves in with you, you won't have to be going back and forth all the time."

"That's true to some degree," Nancy explained. "We'll still have her house to take care of. I really don't want to sell it until she can't remember it. I want to take her home for visits when she wants to go. The doctors tell us that at some point she'll have to go into a locked skilled nursing center. No one can care for an Alzheimer's patient at home once the disease progresses to a point they and the people in the house aren't safe. Harry has already installed a lock high on the doors hoping she won't go outside to wander while we sleep."

"Your Harry is a prince," Lavern said wistfully, wondering if Charlie would ever help her out as much as Harry helped Nancy.

"Should we light a lantern?" Elise asked. If they needed to step away from the fire it was dark.

"No, Mom, let's watch the fire. It's enough," Jolene told her. "Hey, who's that?"

Two figures were approaching their fire.

Nancy pointed her flashlight. "It's Bristol."

"No, I mean, who's with her?"

Bristol and a tall man in jeans, long-sleeved tee shirt, and a ball cap came into their camp fire circle. The man carried two folding chairs in one hand and a guitar case in his other hand.

"Hey everyone," Bristol announced while the man set the guitar case down and began unfolding the chairs. "This is Bud Fisher. He's going to sing and play for us. Bud, this is Elise Parker, her daughter Jolene, Nancy Reynolds, and Lavern Smith." Bristol pointed to each person in turn.

Oh, brother, Elise thought. *This means Bristol will be singing, too. Bristol thinks she can sing much better than she really can. One good thing, she doesn't sing very loud.*

Lavern wondered whether Bristol was looking for a new man in her life, one who would both trail ride and sing with her. Her husband, Richard, was patient, thoughtful, and very good to her. He was not musically inclined, and although he did not ride, he did enjoy the horse. Bristol should count her blessings. It would be hard to find another good man who would put up with her.

Bud nodded and said, "Hey." He sat down, opened his guitar

case, and took out a rather beat up Alvarez guitar. "I've got a Martin at home, but I don't bring it camping," he told the group as he strummed a chord and checked the tuning.

After a couple of adjustments with the tuning knobs, Bud played some introductory chords and began singing "Down in the Valley." Bristol chimed in with some low harmony, leaning toward Bud as they sang. Her short hair spiked two inches high, her large hoop earrings caught the fire light, her scoop-neck tee shirt showed three inches of cleavage, and her thighs strained the fabric of her knee-length shorts.

"Oh, that was good," Bristol gushed. "Do another one."

" 'Down in the Valley' was recorded by Edie Arnold and Burl Ives," Bud informed the group.

"Yes, that's right," Bristol agreed.

Bud played and sang old cowboy songs for over an hour. Bristol joined in on most of them. On the rest of them, it seemed to the women that she just moved her lips pretending to know the words.

After "Ghost Riders in the Sky," Bud put his guitar back in the case. "My voice is giving out," he explained. "Anyway, 'Ghost Riders' was recorded by a few people, Johnny Cash being the most popular."

"Yes, that's right," Bristol agreed.

"So how did all you gals get together? Are you from an OHC club?"

Ohio Horsemen Council was a state wide association consisting of individual county chapters.

"Not really," Nancy told him. "Some of them belong to Portage County OHC, but actually I met each of them at Walmart."

"Huh?" Bud pushed his ball cap back to scratch his head.

"Oh, don't ask!" Bristol groaned.

Lavern gestured toward herself and said, "She met me because we were both in the same aisle when this bozo comes along pushing his cart and eating a Walmart donut. He crumpled the donut bag, threw it on the floor, and kept going. We knew he had no intention of paying for it. We looked at each other and burst out laughing. It wasn't funny that he was essentially stealing from the store. What we found funny was that he had powdered sugar all over his mouth, chin, and nose. It was a dead giveaway that he ate that donut. We started talking, discovered that we both have horses and like camping, and we've been friends ever since."

"For me it was when ...," Elise started to say, but Jolene interrupted her.

"Mom," three syllables this time, "don't tell that story!"

"Well, OK." Elise did not want to embarrass her daughter. "Bud, do you want a S'more?"

"Ah, no, I think I'll check my horse and turn in for the night. I want to ride early in the morning. Hey, do you gals want to come along? I know this whole area really well. Been ridin' here for thirty years, ever since I was a kid. I'll take you some places off park trails that I bet you haven't been."

"That would be awesome," Bristol answered for everyone. "What time?"

"Let's be saddled up ready to ride by eight o'clock," Bud said. When Bristol groaned, he added, "If you're late sleepers, how about eight thirty?"

"Nine o'clock," Jolene said emphatically.

Everyone looked at her, surprised, but no one challenged her. They said their good nights to Bud and he left them sitting at the fire.

"So how did you and Nancy meet?" Lavern asked Elise.

With Bud gone, Jolene did not object to the telling of the story.

"Well, Jolene and I were in Walmart in the aisle for women's products. A young, red-headed stock boy came along with an older, grandmotherly woman, who was practically pulling him down the aisle. She told him she needed help picking out the right tampon. His face was as red as his hair. Nancy came along about then when that woman asked the stock boy, 'What size do you think I am?' "

"The stock boy managed to choke out, 'Ma'am, you better ask these ladies,' and he fled. I think Jolene was almost as red as he was, but Nancy and I had a hard time not laughing in front of that poor woman. She was buying tampons for her granddaughter who was the same height. She never used the products and she really thought size mattered. We got her straightened out, and when she left, Nancy and I started talking. We discovered we both liked horses and did horse camping, and we've been planning trips together ever since."

"That's right," Bristol added as though she had been there herself.

When no one else had anything to add to the conversation around the fire, Bristol went to check on her horse. Elise sent Jolene to check on theirs, and she helped Lavern put away the makings of the S'mores. Nancy folded everyone's lawn chair and leaned them against a tree. When all the horses were tended, and the camp fire burned to coals, the women went to bed, tired and relaxed.

****

By seven in the morning, all the women were up except Bristol and Jolene. The early risers fed and watered their horses and mucked under the picket lines. By the time breakfast was ready, Bristol and Jolene were up. The women ate, then packed their lunches for the trail. Nancy, Elise, and Lavern cleaned up the outdoor kitchen area, while Bristol took care of her horse. Everyone hurried so they could begin grooming and saddling their horses.

"Here, Honey, I bought you a new helmet yesterday at the tack shop up the road."

"Thanks, Mom. When did you do that?" Jolene was over complaining about wearing a helmet.

"After I woke up from my nap, while you were still sleeping yesterday. Wear it in good health and safety."

Bud walked over to see if they were ready to go. His horse, Rocky, a tall, black, Tennessee Walker, was saddled and standing on the picket line, one back foot cocked.

Everyone quickly did their last minute preparations and they all mounted up. It was only five minutes after nine when they left camp. Bud led the way followed by Bristol, then Jolene, Elise, Nancy, and Lavern. Bud rode down the hill from camp, stopping at the stream at the bottom to let the horses drink. He followed the blue trail to the first river crossing.

"The water's kind of high here, but it isn't real swift. I think we can cross,'" Bud told the ladies. He moved Rocky down the incline and into the river. The women watched him until he was halfway across. It looked safe enough, so one by one they moved their mounts into the water. It was deep enough that they had to take their feet out of their stirrups to keep them dry, but the horses did not have to swim.

When Lacy climbed out of the water onto the rocky shore, she started to buck.

"Hang on, Lavern!" Elise called.

"Oh, my gosh!" Nancy said, worried.

Jolene covered her open mouth with her hand, shocked.

Bud and Bristol had moved on down the trail.

Lacy gave one more little buck, then shuddered. Lavern had managed to stay on Lacy's back, to everyone's relief.

Nancy pointed. "Lavern, there's water dripping from your girth. I think it was tickling Lacy's belly making her buck. Good grief!"

"Ride um, cowgirl," Jolene said, impressed. Elise was pleased to hear her add, "Hey, it's a good thing you were wearing your helmet in case you did come off."

The group soon caught up to Bud and Bristol who had paused at a T-intersection at the top of a small rise. Park land was to the right. Bud turned left.

"Isn't this private land?" Nancy asked Bud.

"It's all right. Stay with me. I have a pass."

Bud did take them on trails where they had never before ridden. The scenery was beautiful, winding through hardwood and pine forest, past rock crops and ferns. Sometimes Bud led them off trail to cut over to another. Then they had to duck branches and be careful that their knees did not knock into the trees that were growing so close together.

Suddenly, Bud veered off the trail again to climb a steep hillside. Rocky began galloping up the hill. The other horses started to run, too. Bud was followed by Bristol, then Lavern, Nancy, Jolene, and Elise. Part way up the hill, Lavern's girth strap broke, and her saddle slipped sideways. Lavern was riding on the side of her galloping horse, clinging to the breast collar with her left hand, and to the back of the saddle with her right hand. The saddle was suspended between the breast collar and the crupper. Lavern was terrified of falling and hitting the ground at this speed. She was also terrified that if she fell, she would be trampled by Beauty, Trick and Tucker, the three horses behind her who were moving too fast to stop in time.

They all reached the top of the hill, Lavern still riding the side of her horse. Lacy stopped behind Rocky and Hot Stuff, and Lavern eased herself to the ground, shaking.

"Honey, are you all right?" Nancy asked her. "Geez, I tried to stop Beauty so that if you fell off, we wouldn't run over you, but I couldn't pull her up. She was so determined to keep up with the other horses." Nancy dismounted and put her arms around Lavern.

Bud and Bristol, who had ridden a few yards down the trail, rode back to where the others were congregated at the top of the hill. "What happened?" Bristol asked.

"Look. My girth strap broke. It was only the breast collar and crupper keeping me on my horse," Lavern explained.

"Well, why don't you check out your tack before you ride? Don't you keep your leathers oiled?" Lavern was now going to hold up the ride until a repair could be made, and Bristol was not happy.

"Let me have a look," Bud said, dismounting. "Here, Bristol, hold my horse." He handed her his reins.

Bud saw a way to do a temporary fix to hold the girth in place. He went to his saddlebags and took out a short leather strap and a double-ended brass snap. He walked back to Lacy who was munching grass contentedly.

Just as Bud finished with his repair, Bristol barked, "Come get your own darn horse. He's milling around and it's hard to hold him."

Bud ignored her and told Lavern that he thought the repair would do until she could have a permanent repair made. He offered Lavern a leg up, then Nancy. When he swung back on his saddle, the group started off again at a controlled walk.

The group rode for another hour before Bud had them back on park land. They stopped on the top of a hill on the yellow trail where the park had strung a high line. They picketed their horses, pulled out their packed lunches and water bottles, and settled themselves on a log to eat.

"Lavern, what are you trying to do today, prove that you can do trick riding and ride bucking broncos? You've been giving us a scare." Elise took a bite of her sandwich.

"Yes, I'm a cowgirl of many talents, but I don't think I like using them." Lavern crunched a carrot stick.

"Those really were beautiful places you took us to this morning, Bud," Bristol said, leaning toward him. "When will you be coming to Beaver Creek again?"

"I come 'most every weekend. I live really close," he told her.

"Good to know," she said.

After lunch, the group rode for another hour before returning to camp. There would be no nap time today. They were going to pack up and break camp to go home. Bristol finished first and walked off to find Bud and sing a few more songs with him.

"Hey, Nancy, how did you meet Bristol?" Lavern asked her.

"Yeah, tell us another Walmart story," Jolene said.

Elise put down her manure fork and drew up a chair. "Yeah, I want to hear this, too."

They all sat down under Nancy's awning. "Well, yes, it was in Walmart where I met her. I needed to use the restroom, and apparently, so did Bristol. We went into the store restroom at the same time. There was a woman in one of the stalls calling for help. Bristol asked her what was wrong. She said she was stuck on the toilet seat. I expected to find a hugely overweight woman wedged onto the seat, but when we opened the door (and thank goodness the door opened outward instead of inward), here was this normal size, middle-aged woman with tears running down her cheeks that were red with embarrassment. I asked her what was wrong, and she said it felt like the seat was glued to her bottom, that she couldn't get up without it pulling and hurting her skin. Bristol was very gentle with her and talked to her in a soothing way. We tried to help her up, but she screamed in pain. I said I would go for help, and Bristol volunteered to stay with her to keep her calm until help came.

"How embarrassing! I can't imagine!" Jolene said.

"Yes, the embarrassment would be worse than the pain," Lavern agreed.

"So what happened to that poor lady?" Elise asked.

"Well, Bristol must have figured that I would come back with help in the masculine form. She was right, of course. So, anyway, Bristol had taken off her jacket and put it on this lady's lap to kind of cover her. I thought that was thoughtful of her. I had two men with me. They checked out the situation, then left to get a couple of tools. Bristol and I stayed with her and talked about normal things trying to keep her calm. That's when I discovered Bristol was into horses. When the men returned, they had called 911. Before the paramedics came, the guys had used the tools to take the seat off of the commode. That seat was stuck to her butt, all right. The paramedics took her to the hospital with that thing still on her backside. By then, of course, Bristol and I had exchanged names and phone numbers."

"Wow, that poor lady," said Jolene.

"Yeah, she was mortified, all right. Later we heard on the news that someone had put super glue on the toilet seats in that Walmart. I guess the lady sat down before it had dried. So, anyway, Bristol and I did a few day rides together shortly after that. I had only known her a couple of months when Bright Beauty had colic. I was frantic. I walked Beauty for an hour and she seemed worse instead of better. I called the vet, then I called Bristol. She was at my barn before the vet arrived. I know Bristol can be a pistol, but you know, girls, there's some good in every one. With some people you just have to look harder. And remember, it can be the meanest people who hurt inside the most. I don't know why she's so unhappy that she lashes out, but I think she's very insecure for some reason. Try not to take it personally. And remember, part of the Lord's Prayer is to forgive others so that we can be forgiven of our own mistakes."

Jolene was thoughtful. "Wow," she said.

"Umm," murmured Lavern, unable to think of toxic Bristol in a positive light.

Huh, Elise, thought, *this is a good lesson for all of us, but forgiveness is very hard. Bristol the pistol, indeed.*

"Come on girls. Let's get these awnings down and the horses loaded. We have husbands waiting at home."

"Yeah, not to mention problems," Lavern said.

"Right, not to mention problems," Nancy said kindly, although they all knew she was willing to listen anytime, as she had often done in the past.

They finished breaking camp, loaded all the horses, and said good-bye to Bud. They were ready to caravan home to Portage County, about a two-hour trip, first on country roads, then north on Route 11.

After only twenty minutes of travel on the highway, there was a loud bang, and Elise's truck began to swerve. "Hang on, Honey," she told Jolene. "This could be bad!"

"I'm OK, Mom, you just drive. You can do it." Jolene had a death grip on the arm rest.

Elise guessed that the truck had blown a tire. The whole rig was swerving back and forth, and Elise was afraid that the rig would jackknife, or that the trailer with the horses would roll over, maybe even rolling the truck. She lifted her foot from the accelerator instead of using the brakes.

Lavern, who was driving right behind Elise, heard the loud

bang and saw huge pieces of rubber tire flying through the air. She began braking gently as she watched Elise's rig swaying side to side. *Oh please keep them safe,* she prayed as her rig slowed behind Elise's.

Elise gently steered through the swerves and the rig began to slow. Finally she was able to guide it onto the berm. When the truck finally came to a stop, Elise put her head in her hands over the steering wheel. Jolene let go of her tight grip on the arm rest, reached for her cell phone, and called the American Automobile Association.

"Here, Mom, talk to Triple A." Jolene handed her mother the phone. Elise pulled herself together and explained her problem. Jolene dug in her mother's purse for the membership card and handed it to her. When arrangements were made, Elise told Jolene it would be at least two hours until help would arrive.

Nancy, who was in the lead, had pulled over and carefully backed up. Lavern and Bristol, who were following Elise, had slowed down as she did, and pulled onto the shoulder behind her. They all got out of their trucks and stood looking at the damage. Elise had indeed blown a tire. Pieces of it were all over the highway. Elise told the group that she and Jolene would be stuck here for more than two hours waiting for help.

"Well, I've got cheese and crackers," Bristol announced.

"I have iced tea and lemonade," Nancy told them.

"I have a deck of cards," said Lavern.

"We all have folding chairs," added Nancy.

"We have our folding table," said Jolene.

Elise shook her head at her friends, grateful that they were going to stay with her until the problem was fixed. She checked on the horses that were contentedly munching hay from the hanging bags inside the trailer, blissfully unaware of the potential tragedy that could have happened.

The women set up the table and chairs on the grass at the side of the highway. Food and drinks were passed around, and the cards were dealt. Traffic whizzed by them at 65 and 70 miles per hour as they made the most of it while waiting for life to get better.

CHAPTER 2
NANCY

On Saturday morning, Nancy took a last look around the newly painted spare bedroom. The walls were now pale lavender, her mother's favorite color. The new comforter on top of the bed had a lavender and white print. A lavender stuffed puppy snuggled in the pillows. The white pillow cases had eyelet edge trim. Curtains at the window were white eyelet. An eight by ten framed photograph of her mother and father on their fiftieth anniversary sat on top of the dresser. Nancy hoped her mother would enjoy the room.

"Harry, I'm going to pick up Mom now. We can have lunch when I get home. Thanks again for painting this room. Sis did a nice job picking out the curtains and bedding. The puppy's a nice touch. It all looks great."

They stood together in the doorway, arms around each other's waist. Harry bent to kiss the top of Nancy's head. "Yes, it does look good. I see a couple places I need to touch up, but I think your mother will like this. Are you sure you don't want me to go along?"

"No, I can handle her. I know you want to work in the garden. Oh, would you cut some zinnias and put them in a vase in here? I meant to do that this morning." Nancy looked up into her husband's handsome face.

"Sure, Honey. Just get the vase out for me. I don't know where you keep them. Put it on the kitchen counter, and I'll have the flowers in here in time for her arrival. And Sweetie, don't worry about this. It'll work out." He patted her cheek and smiled his reassurance.

Nancy felt blessed to have such an understanding husband. "OK, then, I'm gone." She kissed Harry on his lips, squeezed him in a bear hug, and walked down the hall to the door leading to the garage attached to their ranch-style home. She grabbed her keys from the hook as she wondered if they would now have to hide the keys from her mother, since she would be living with them.

Nancy drove her red Kia sedan the twenty minutes to her mother's two-story frame house. She knocked at the door, but no one answered. She used her key to enter and found her mother, Mary, in the kitchen. Mary's face and arms were streaked in black.

"Mom! What is all over your face and arms?" Nancy grabbed Mary's arms and held them out to inspect. "What in the world is this?" She touched her mother's face.

Mary did not answer. She patted her chest and smiled.

Nancy noticed that her mother's bosom seemed to be padded beyond its natural size. "Mom, what is this?" Nancy pulled at her mother's blue top and discovered that Mary had been stuffing newspapers inside her clothing. The ink had rubbed off onto her face and arms. "Oh, Mom, you have ink all over you. Why are you wearing newspapers? Come on, let's get you cleaned up."

Nancy began to take the newspapers out, but Mary squirmed and protested. "OK, Mom, tell you what. How would you like to come visit Harry and me? You could stay all night. We could eat popcorn and have a slumber party. Want to?"

Mary nodded yes. "OK, then," Nancy told her, "we need to pack some clothes for you. Look, I brought a suitcase. What would you like to put in it? Let's go look in your closet."

Mary led the way to her bedroom upstairs. She helped Nancy pick out clothes. Mary did not seem to realize that they were packing many more clothes than were needed for one overnight. When the bag was fully packed, Nancy led her mother to the bathroom where she was able to remove the newspapers and to help her mother wash off the ink.

"OK, Mom, you look good now. Let's go. Should we stop by Walmart on our way? You enjoy looking around there."

"Let's go to Walmart! I like to go to Walmart." Mary started down the stairs and Nancy lugged the suitcase down the steps behind her.

Nancy thought she would have to go next door to see Karen Nettle who watched over Mary for her, helped her to dress each morning, and made sure she had a good breakfast, but Karen was just coming up Mary's walk. "Hi, Karen, I was just going to come over to settle up with you for this past week."

"Hi, Nancy. Thanks. I could use the money. I'll miss taking care of your mother every morning. It really gave me something to do, and besides, I have always liked Mary. She was a wonderful neighbor, kind and caring. I hate that she got that old timer's disease."

The two women hugged on the front sidewalk. Nancy handed Karen a check.

"Now, you know you can call me if you need me to watch her

for awhile if you and your sweet husband need to go away. I wouldn't mind making the twenty minute trip over to help out. It would give me a chance to see my Mary again, plus make a little money." Karen turned to Mary who was standing on the grass staring at a butterfly. "Goodbye, Mary. Be good." She hugged her.

Mary pulled out of the hug. "We're going to Walmart!"

"Well, you have a good time, Dear. I know you love to shop at Walmart."

Nancy buckled the seat belt around her mother and loaded the suitcase into the trunk of the Kia. Soon they were half way to the Walmart. At a red light in a busy intersection, Mary opened the car door and began to get out.

"Mom, what are you doing? Shut the door! You can't get out here! We're not there yet! Shut the door!"

The light turned green, horns blared, and Mary struggled to exit the car against the restraint of her seat belt. Nancy was about to get out to go around to the passenger side, when she thought of saying, "Mom, if you don't shut the door right now, we can't go to Walmart. The car won't take us there with the door open."

Mary quit struggling against the seat belt and shut the door. Relieved, Nancy drove off. This time she not only locked the doors, but she activated the child lock on the passenger side door.

They arrived at Walmart and made the rounds of the aisles without another incident until they came to an end-cap display of chewing gum at the checkout counter. Mary began to pick up packs of gum and stuff them into her blouse. Nancy tried to stop her, but her mother squealed and pushed her away. Nancy was embarrassed as people were beginning to look.

"Mom, you look all lumpy with that gum down your front. Let's take it out, and I'll buy some for you."

Mary continued to stuff the gum inside of her clothing. Nancy took her arm to stop her. Mary screamed, "I want it! I want it! It's mine!"

A store manager came over and stood with arms folded across his chest, a scowl on his face. He was unsure what to do. He realized that Nancy was trying to work with Mary and correct the situation.

"OK, Mom, it's yours, but we have to put it over here, or the alarm will ring, and they'll take it away from you. Here, I'll help you put it on the belt, and then we can take it home."

Mary finally allowed the gum to go onto the conveyor belt. Nancy said to the check-out girl that she only wanted one pack of each flavor. "Can you put the others aside while I distract my mother?"

The young girl with pink hair, an eyebrow ring, nose ring, and probably a belly button ring, nodded while chewing and popping her own gum.

They made it through the check out and into the car. When Nancy pulled into her drive, her mother said wistfully, "You know, I would really like to go to Walmart. I like to go to Walmart. Can we go to Walmart?" Mary patted the purse on her lap.

"Sure, Mom, I'll take you there. Don't you want to eat lunch first?"

"No, I want to go to Walmart." Mary was rubbing her arm, up and down, up and down, in agitation.

"OK, Mom, we'll go for a short trip to Walmart. Then we

need to come back and have lunch. Just let me run in and tell Harry."

Nancy found Harry in the back yard garden pulling weeds. "Honey, I'm taking Mom to Walmart. I plan to make it a short trip. We should be back by noon and I'll fix us some lunch, but go ahead and eat if you get too hungry."

"I thought you were going to stop at Walmart on your way home." Harry brushed a hand across his forehead leaving a streak of dirt. A pile of pulled weeds lay at his feet.

"Well, we did stop, but she doesn't remember, and she keeps saying she wants to go to Walmart, so I'm taking her back." Nancy jingled the keys.

"You're a good daughter. And have I told you lately that you're a good wife? I love you." Harry blew her a kiss.

Nancy blew him a kiss back and smiled. "I love you, too. See you!"

Nancy drove Mary back to Walmart hoping that there would not be another incident. Walmart was only ten minutes away, half-way between her house and her mother's. They strolled the aisles and they were ready to leave the store again when Mary saw a baby in a stroller. She broke free from Nancy's guiding arm to have a closer look.

"Baby! It's a baby! How sweet! My baby!"

At first, the mother smiled at Mary until Mary reached for the baby. The mother quickly turned the stroller around and headed in the other direction as Nancy caught up to Mary and grabbed her arm. "Come on Mom, let's go have lunch. Are you hungry?"

"Yes, I'm hungry. Let's eat lunch," Mary said, distracted.

****

Mary seemed to like her lavender bedroom. After lunch, she lay down on the bed and hugged the lavender puppy.

Nancy emptied the suitcase and hung her mother's clothing in the closet. She kissed her mother's cheek and gently closed the bedroom door as she left.

"I think Mom's going to take a nap," she told Harry. "I'm going to pay some bills online. It takes me twice as long now that I pay ours and hers both. This will be good, uninterrupted time to get it done while she naps."

An hour later, Nancy was finished with the computer. She walked down the hall to check on her mother. When she opened the bedroom door, she was shocked to see the zinnias on the floor and her mother drinking the water from the flower vase.

"Mom! What are you doing?" Nancy just barely kept herself from shouting.

"I was thirsty," her mother told her.

"Come on, let's get you a glass of water." Nancy took the vase from Mary, then led her to the kitchen. She gave her a glass of water and settled her in a chair. She refilled the vase, and then returned to the bedroom for the flowers. Harry was in the living room when she brought in the flowers. "It's a good thing we brought Mom here to live," she told him. "She was drinking the water for the flowers."

Harry shook his head. "We'll keep her here with us as long as we can, Honey, but you know that the day will come when she'll have to go into twenty-four hour care."

"Yes, I realize that, especially after today, but I appreciate you being so good about her being here now. You're the greatest." She gave her husband a quick kiss and went back to the kitchen to check on her mother and to start dinner.

Mary sat in the cheery kitchen with her hands folded on her chest. "I want to go home," she told Nancy.

"Mom, it's not time to go home yet. Do you want a cup of coffee while I start dinner?"

"I don't know. Do I drink coffee? I want to go home now."

"Oh, Mom!" Nancy hugged her mother. "Tell you what. Let's go feed the horse. You haven't seen Bright Beauty yet today. She misses you. Do you want to give her a carrot?" Nancy turned to the refrigerator.

"I don't have a carrot," Mary said wistfully.

"It's OK, Mom, I do. Here's a carrot. Let's go see Beauty. "

Nancy led Mary out the back door to the small two-stall horse barn. Bright Beauty was still inside, out of the hot sun. The horse nickered when they entered the barn. Nancy showed Mary how to feed small bites of carrot to the mare on the flat of her palm so that her fingers would not be nipped.

"Pretty!" Mary remarked of the palomino mare. She rubbed Beauty's neck. The horse nosed Mary for more carrot. Mary laughed.

"Mom, would you like to brush her?"

Mary nodded.

"All right, then. You stand over here and don't move so I can take her out of the stall. I don't want her to step on your foot.

That hurts!" Nancy opened the stall door and led Beauty to the cross ties. She opened the tack box and pulled out a brush. "Mom, like this, nice and gentle."

Nancy observed while Mary brushed the fox trotter mare. It seemed to have a calming effect on Mary and Nancy was pleased. Unless she could somehow manage her chores while watching her mother, there would be many things she would no longer be able to do. She could already see that having her mother live with her was going to be very time consuming.

****

On Sunday, Nancy and Harry took Mary to their church with them. Nancy had baked a cake for her contribution to the pot luck meal that would follow the service today. Mary sang the familiar hymns and was quiet during the prayer and scripture reading. But when the minister droned on and on during a too-long sermon, Mary suddenly stood up and shouted, "Enough of this! I know this stuff. Let's go eat!"

An embarrassed Nancy tugged at Mary's dress, but Mary pulled free and exited the pew with Nancy and Harry hurrying down the aisle after her. The minister stopped speaking as the congregation laughed good naturedly. Then in groups of two, three, and four, the people stood up and followed the Reynolds to the church basement for the meal. The organist took her cue from the congregation and played the final hymn as everyone marched out, laughing and talking.

****

Busy days passed by for Nancy as she cared for her mother,

her home, and her horse. Harry helped out as much as he could, but he had a full-time job as a computer analyst. He fed Bright Beauty in the evening, turned her out and cleaned the stall. In the summer Beauty stayed outside in the pasture during the evenings and overnight while the temperatures were cooler. In the late mornings, Nancy brought her inside and fed her. Beauty remained inside the cooler barn during the hot days.

Harry was up at six o'clock to get ready for work. Nancy had always been able to make him breakfast, pack his lunch, and kiss him goodbye. She enjoyed waving from the door as he drove off. Now, with her mother sapping her time and energy, she was having difficulty with this morning routine. Mary would usually be up between six and six-thirty. It was difficult for Nancy to manage helping her while getting Harry ready.

This morning, Mary joined them in the kitchen while Harry was eating his breakfast, and Nancy was making his sandwich.

"Mom, I see you dressed yourself. You can come in here with your robe until I can help you with that. You have your clothes on inside out." Nancy poured her mother a cup of coffee and tried not to laugh. Mary's clothes not only were inside out, but she was also wearing her bra on the outside of her blouse.

"What do you want for breakfast? Cereal?"

"I want to go to Walmart."

"Ok, Mom. First things first. Here are your pills. You can take them with this coffee."

"No, I took my pills." Mary pushed them away.

"No, Mom. You didn't. You just got up. You just came in here. Come on, take your pills."

"No!"

"Mom, come on. I need you to take your medicine so I can finish making Harry's lunch." Nancy put a banana in front of her mother.

Mary picked up the banana and tucked it into her bra. She reached over and took the banana meant for Harry's lunch and tucked it into the other side of her bra.

"I want to go to Walmart."

Nancy pictured Mary at Walmart dressed this way with bananas poking out of the bra worn outside of her blouse and grinned. She glanced at Harry, and they both laughed.

Nancy finished packing Harry's lunch, put his breakfast dishes in the sink, gave her mother a bowl of cereal, and tried again to have her mother take her medicine.

"No!"

"Mom, you need this. Come on. Please don't argue this morning."

"I want to go to Walmart."

"OK. Tell you what. I need some groceries. We can get them at Walmart today, but you have to take your pills first. We can't go until you do."

After several more minutes of argument, Mary finally took her pills as Harry was ready to leave.

Nancy walked to the door with Harry.

"Thanks for the breakfast and the lunch, Honey." He kissed Nancy good-bye.

"Have a good day, Harry." Nancy waved from the door until Harry drove out of sight. When she turned back to the kitchen, she saw that Mary was taking all the pots and pans out of her cupboard.

"What are you doing, Mom?" Pans were on the floor, the counter, and the table. "Stop, Mom. What are you doing?"

"Spring cleaning."

"Don't you want to go to Walmart? We can't go and leave these all over. Help me put them back. No, never mind. I'll put them back."

It took several minutes for Nancy to fit the pots and pans back into the cupboards.

"I need to shower and get dressed now, Mom. Do you want to watch TV?"

"I want to go to Walmart."

"I know you do. We will. Today." Nancy led her mother into the living room and turned on the television. "You watch TV and let me get ready. Please just sit here, and don't do anything."

Nancy jumped into the shower, quickly finished, and dressed in a hurry. She was relieved to see her mother still sitting in the chair watching the television. "OK, Mom. Let's change your clothes. Come on." She led Mary into the bedroom.

"I want to wear this." The two bananas still protruded from Mary's bra.

"You can, Mom. We just want to put your underwear on the inside next to you." Nancy reached for the bananas. Mary protested and turned away. "All right, then, Mom. You take off your clothes while I make your bed."

When Nancy pulled back the bedcovers to straighten them, she found a pile of fruit that Mary had hidden there. Rather than upset Mary who was undressing, she made the bed with the fruit still under the covers. She handed Mary her bra to put back on and turned Mary's blouse and slacks right side out, then helped Mary put them on again over her underwear. She brushed her mother's hair. "OK, you're ready for Walmart now. Let's go so we can be back in time to bring Bright Beauty into the barn and give her breakfast."

They were all the way to Walmart when Nancy realized that she had not had time to eat her own breakfast this morning. Nancy led Mary inside.

"We need a cart, Mom. I have to buy groceries for the week. Please hold on to the cart and don't let go." Nancy hoped holding onto the cart might keep her mother out of trouble.

In the produce section, Nancy looked for bananas that were not too green. She chose a bunch and turned to put them into the cart. Mary was gone.

"Mom!" Nancy called. She turned in a circle to look for her. Mary was just turning the corner at the end of the isle. Nancy left the cart and hurried to catch up to her.

"This way, Mom. We have to buy some apples." Nancy took Mary's arm and led her back to the cart in produce.

"I don't want an apple."

"That's all right, Mom. They're for later, and for Bright Beauty. Don't you want to feed the horse?"

"Yes, the horse can eat the apples."

"Good, Mom. First, how about these carrots? We can put them in our salads and Beauty likes them, too."

"Yes, the horse can eat the carrots." Mary began putting bunches of carrots into the cart.

"No, Mom, no. We only need two bunches. Help me put these back."

They moved down the aisle to the apples. As Nancy bagged golden delicious she wondered which was more difficult, shopping with her mother or shopping with a two year old. Turning to place the bagged apples into the cart, Nancy saw Mary's blouse lying on top of the carrots. Mary was standing there in her bra.

"What? Oh, Mom, no!" Nancy grabbed the blouse and spun her mother around. "Here, put this back on. Quick!"

"It's hot," Mary complained.

"I don't care. You still can't go around without your blouse. Stick your arm in here."

Roy, the red haired stock boy, was just coming out of the back room. When he saw Mary in her underwear, his face turned nearly as red as his hair. Mary winked at him.

Distracted by Roy, Mary allowed Nancy to help her put her blouse back on.

Roy was backing up, keeping his cart of produce between himself and Mary.

"Come here, Honey. Give me a kiss and a hug." Mary winked at Roy again.

"Quiet!" Nancy ordered her mother while buttoning the blouse. "I'm sorry," she said to the stock boy. "She has

Alzheimer's. I'll watch her more closely."

Nancy finished the shopping as quickly as she could and drove home. She was trying to put away the groceries while keeping an eye on her mother when her cell phone rang. It was Bristol.

"Hi, Nancy. Guess what? I went to the open mic at the Amped Up last night and sang harmony with some of the guys. It was great! The people just loved us! We got so much applause. They wanted us to sing more songs. They…"

"Bristol, I'm sorry. I just don't have time to talk. My mother is here with us now, and she's a real handful. I'm so tired I don't know if I found a rope or lost my horse." Mary had left the kitchen, and Nancy began to walk through the house looking for her while she talked to Bristol.

"Well, really, I thought you would be happy for me," Bristol said indignantly.

Nancy found her mother in her bedroom dressing the lavender puppy with layers of freshly folded clothes from the laundry.

"Bristol, I'm sorry. I'm busy here. Gotta go." Nancy hung up to rescue the clean laundry, put the groceries away, tend to her horse, and make lunch for herself and her mother.

****

That evening while Mary was watching the television, Nancy called her sister to confirm that she would definitely be here to watch their mother so that Nancy could go on the June horse campout with her friends. "Sis, it isn't easy doing this day after day. I'm so tired! It's hard to get much done. I haven't ridden Bright Beauty since Mom's been here. I can't leave Mom for

Harry to handle alone. I appreciate you coming so I can go. Thank you ever so much!"

After hanging up, Nancy called Bristol back. "Bristol, you wouldn't believe the amount of time and energy it takes looking after my mother. I'm not sure this is going to work out having her here. I really hate the idea of putting her into a home, though."

"So why are you calling me about it? You didn't have time for me when I called you earlier today, so why should I listen to you now?" Bristol hung up.

"Because I was calling to explain and to apologize," Nancy said into the empty phone. *Dear Lord,* Nancy prayed, *Please give me strength and patience to deal with my mother, and please help Bristol to release her anger issues. Amen.*

As Nancy offered her quick prayer, Mary left the living room. Harry took the opportunity to talk with Nancy.

"Come here and sit down with me," Harry said to her. "I have an idea to discuss with you." Harry understood the stress that Nancy was under.

Nancy sat on the couch beside her husband who put his arm around her shoulders. She put her head on his chest. He stroked her hair. "Why don't you call your mother's neighbor, what's her name, Karen somebody."

"Karen Nettle."

"Yeah, Karen, to have her come over here for two or three hours a day, maybe three or four days a week to be with your mother and do things for her? Would that give you enough help? Use her more if she'll do it."

"I don't know. We would have to pay her. How much can we

afford?"

"How much would it cost us for you to wear out and become sick? How much is peace of mind worth?"

"Harry, you're wonderful! I'm so glad you understand what this is like for me. I'll call Karen now. Even if she could come only once a week to stay while I grocery shop, it would be a huge help." Nancy kissed her husband and jumped up to make the call.

Before she finished dialing, she smelled something burning. She ran into the kitchen where she found the microwave timer set on thirty minutes and popcorn burning inside.

"Oh, Mom," Nancy said as she shut off the microwave and threw out the popcorn. "Let me make you some fresh popcorn."

CHAPTER 3
BRISTOL

Bristol frowned as she accepted the report from Tracie Gold. "I hope this is a better job than the last one you did," she told her. "Did you do a spell check?"

Tracie frowned back at the office manager no one liked, and blew a wisp of her blond hair from her eyes. A good day at work was a day when Bristol had taken a vacation or a sick day from the company that handled payroll, taxes, accounting, and financial planning.

"Yes, I spell checked. I think it's OK," she answered meekly. Tracie did not feel meek, but she had found pretending to be meek a useful way to deal with this unreasonable woman.

"Well, you should know and not just think. I'll read it over to correct your mistakes before I hand it in. Go work on the time sheets." Bristol waved the petite young girl away. She knew that Tracie did good work, but she liked to keep all the office staff on their toes. They had college degrees in finance and accounting and were certified public accountants, while Bristol had worked her way up from secretary to office manager with a high school diploma, seniority, and schmoozing the boss. Bristol was not as confident as she portrayed. She was intimidated by the college degrees. She felt that to advance her position, or even to keep it, she needed to be a player in the game of office politics.

Bristol's cell phone rang. She dug it out of her purse.

Checking the number, she saw that it was her husband, Richard, calling. "What?" she asked Ric impatiently.

Ric told her that he had arranged to pick up their granddaughter immediately after work, and that he was headed there now. He finished his job in sales at four o'clock, an hour before Bristol's quitting time.

"Well, you can just turn around and forget that. This is Wednesday, not Monday, so we don't have to have her tonight. Anyway, we have plans to go to the movies."

"I can't disappoint her now. She'll be watching for me. We can take her to a show with us."

"Look, I don't want to go see some dumb Disney kids' flick, so if that's what you want, go ahead. I'll be home later." Bristol clicked her phone shut. *Fine*, she thought. This would give her a chance to go to the open mic at the Amped Up. They served sandwiches and fries, so she could eat supper there and wait for the music to begin. Maybe someone she knew would be there, and she could sing harmony with them.

At five o'clock, Bristol grabbed her purse and headed for the door. The other office personnel were getting ready to leave, telling each other goodbye and to have a nice evening. No one spoke to Bristol, and Bristol spoke to no one.

The temperature was still in the 80's, and Bristol switched on the air conditioning after starting her blue Toyota Camry. She checked her spiked hair and her make up in the rear view mirror before pulling out of the parking lot. She was dressed professionally in brown slacks with a brown and black lightweight tweed jacket, cream blouse, and gold earrings and bracelet. She seldom wore skirts because she did not like displaying her pudgy legs. Her ankles were too thick to look good in heels, so she wore a pair of dressy sandals.

There were only a few people in the Amped Up when Bristol arrived, but by the time she finished her sandwich, it had begun to fill up with others who came to eat, listen to music, and maybe to sing.

Two microphones were connected to amplifiers set up on a stage in a back room at the rear of the bar. Bristol looked around, but she did not see anyone she knew. It was still a half hour until the open mic would begin, so she struck up a conversation with two men sitting at the next table drinking beer from long neck bottles. When she found out that they did not sing, she shut down the conversation and ignored them.

Finally, Ernie, the emcee, hopped up on stage to welcome the audience and the musicians. "Make sure that you're on the signup sheet if you want to perform," he told them. "We'll start in about five minutes."

Bristol did not sign the list. She wanted to sing harmony, not solo, and she could not play a guitar. A singer needed accompaniment. Someday she would have to buy a guitar and learn to play it. She noticed that most of the musicians who sang country songs had a Martin guitar. She had already researched the Martin brand and had decided that was what she wanted.

Ernie began calling the musicians to the stage. The first was a tall, beautiful, young woman with long, black hair, wearing a slinky black dress. She sang a blues ballad, and the crowd applauded long and hard for her sultry, bluesy voice. Next was an old hippie-type man wearing a tee shirt with a peace sign over his large belly, and gray hair pulled into a pony tail. He sang an original song that brought enthusiastic applause from the audience and hoots from his friends. Another man sang a John Denver song, and a woman sang one by Christina Aguilera.

Then a man in cowboy boots and hat, blue jeans, and western shirt came to the mic. He carried a battered guitar. Bristol thought this guy had possibilities. When the cowboy started to sing George Strait's *Amarillo By Morning* in a rich tenor voice, Bristol joined him on stage at the second mic, uninvited. She knew all the words to this song, and she sang a low harmony. She did not notice the odd look he gave her. The song brought only polite applause.

As Bristol left the stage in front of him, she turned back, looked up at him and introduced herself. He nodded, but said nothing, and returned to his seat. She was disappointed because she thought they had sounded good together. He certainly had a good voice, and she felt that her harmony added depth to the song.

Bristol sang a few more songs with three other men, joining them on stage, uninvited, before she decided to go home. Tomorrow was another work day, and it would come early.

****

Thursday morning, the office air conditioning was running on the cold side, and Bristol was grateful for the turquoise jacket she was wearing with her black slacks and white blouse. Her silver and turquoise earrings could easily be seen below her short, spiked, bleached-blond hair. She was reading Tracie's report. It was well written and although she tried, Bristol could not find fault with it. Bristol had heard Tracie saying things about her to the other women in the office, and so she had marked Tracie as a troublemaker. The other women had agreed with Tracie's negative comments about Bristol, but it was Tracie who started the gossip. Bristol would deal with the others later, but Tracie was first on her list.

Each of the five women working here had her own office off of a square area that contained the copier, large table for projects to be spread out, postage meter, and other common-use machines. At the end of a short hall, the restrooms were on the right, and the office of the boss, Larry Brown, was on the left.

"Tracie, come in here," Bristol called out. She moved the two photos of her horse Hot Stuff around her desk top. There were no photos of her family, nor were there any other personal items in her office.

When Tracie entered, Bristol handed her a packet that was ready to be mailed. "I want you to take this to the post office so it goes out right away. Send it priority mail. Go now."

As soon as Tracie left the building, Bristol walked down the hall to talk to the boss. "Larry," she said entering his office, "here's the report I had Tracie work on. I might as well have done it myself considering all the changes I needed to make on it. It should meet with your approval now that I fixed it. Where is she this morning, anyway? I haven't seen her. She's never around when I want her."

Larry sighed and adjusted his navy tie, then held out his hand for the report. He was an older man, wearing a pin-striped business suit, clean-shaven, with gray hair and tired blue eyes. "Your job is to manage the office staff. If you feel that you need to, go ahead and write her up. I don't want to be involved unless it becomes an employment problem."

"Yes, Sir." Bristol responded. She made a quick exit from Larry's office before her boss could catch her smirking. She would not write a formal complaint against Tracie until she had a real one, but hopefully she had planted some seeds in the mind of the boss.

Bristol returned to her office and picked up a box with a large project to copy, compile, hole punch, and bind. She wanted to hand it off to one of the other women, but she knew that they were extra busy at the first of the month working on last month's reports for clients. She could at least start it while Tracie was gone, then maybe assign it to Tracie on her return, putting her in a time bind. If she could create enough stress and pressure on Tracie, maybe Tracie would search for another job.

Bristol carried the heavy box to the common area, and set it on the long table near the copier. She returned to her office for her Sirius radio, set it on the table where she would be working, and cranked up her favorite country music station. She began making copies of the originals in the box. One after the other, office doors slammed shut against the sound of the music. Bristol paid no attention. If she was going to have to do a boring job by rote, she could at least enjoy her music.

****

At the end of the day, Bristol drove the half hour home. She parked her blue Camry in the garage next to her white Ford F250 which she used to pull her horse trailer. The garage was next to the blue ranch-style home with white window shutters. The barn was at the top of a short hill. The tractor and gooseneck trailer were parked beside the barn.

Bristol walked to the pasture fence behind the garage and whistled for Hot Stuff. He looked up from his grazing and bent his head to eat grass again. Bristol shrugged and went into the house. Throwing down her keys on the kitchen counter near the back door, she called to her husband.

"Are you here, Ric?"

He answered from within the house. "Yeah, I'm here, but I'm going outside. I need to mow." He was changing his clothes in the bedroom, putting on his blue jeans and a work shirt. "Hey, come on in here. I have something to show you."

Bristol thought *what now?* She walked into the bedroom, but not because Ric asked her to. She wanted to change out of her dress clothes.

Ric was grinning at her. "Look at this," he said, as he reached down, picked up a guitar case, and set it on top of the bed.

"What's this?" Bristol asked him.

"It's a guitar!" Ric opened the case. Inside was a Martin D1. Ric was still grinning at her.

"I know it's a guitar," Bristol snapped. "What the heck are you doing with it?"

"I bought it for you. It's a gift. I know how badly you want to sing, and I thought you could learn to play it and accompany yourself." He caressed the wood top and plucked a string.

"Well, I *do* sing, and of *course* I could learn to play it." She walked over to the bed and took the guitar out of the case. "It has laminated back and sides. What is it?"

"It's a Martin."

"I can see that," Bristol snapped ungraciously. "Where did you get it? Can you take it back for a Martin D28 or a D18?" She placed the guitar back in the case and snapped it shut.

Ric, no longer smiling, said, "Sure, anything you want. I'll exchange it tomorrow." There was only a trace of sarcasm in his voice. "I'm going out to mow the pasture with the tractor. Can I interest you in learning how to run the lawn tractor so you can mow the yard?"

"No, I'm not going to do that, but I'll bring you out a glass of water later. It's hot."

"Well, thanks for that at least. I have something else to ask you. I have an early sales meeting tomorrow morning. Would you be willing to feed the horse and barn cats to help me make an earlier start tomorrow?" Ric tucked a blue handkerchief into his pocket.

"I already have to get up early for work. I'm not going to get up any earlier." Bristol turned to walk out of the room.

Ric stopped her by saying, "No, you won't do me a favor and feed your own horse for one morning, you won't mow the lawn while I mow the pasture, and you don't appreciate my gift to you. I try pretty hard around here, but I don't see you giving much. Are you planning on making any dinner tonight?"

"It's too hot to eat much. I'll toss a salad, and you can drink a beer with it when you're done mowing. As for the horse, I know you love Hot Stuff and like to fool around with him even though you don't ride. If you don't like the way things are, don't think about leaving. I make more money than you do, and if we have to divide the assets, you won't have nearly as much as you think." Bristol grabbed her shorts and a tee shirt, and headed to the bathroom to change.

When Ric left the house, Bristol took out her cell phone. She and Bud had exchanged phone numbers when they met at Beaver Creek. Up until now, neither had called the other. When she heard the tractor start up, she punched in Bud's number. It reached his voice mail. "Hi, Bud," she said in a throaty voice that she hoped was sexy. "Do you remember that place I told you about with the open mic, the Amped Up? I'm going to be there tomorrow night. Why don't you drive up here and we can sing together. Call me. Oh, and I have a new guitar. Maybe you can show me a few chords." She did not leave her name. He should know who it is.

In the kitchen, Bristol tossed her cell phone onto the counter. She made a salad, set a bowl of it aside for her husband, grabbed a beer, and sat at the counter to eat. She hoped that Bud would call back before Ric was finished mowing. It would be easier to talk with Bud without Ric's big ears listening.

She rinsed her bowl and fork and put them into the dishwasher. She poured a glass of ice water from the pitcher in the refrigerator. Before she could take it outside to Ric, her cell phone rang. She grabbed the phone, checked the number, and said in a breathy voice, "Hello, Bud. How are you?"

"I'm fine. How about you? It was good to hear from you. Have you been doing any riding?"

"Oh, I'm fine. Yeah, I've done a couple of Sunday day rides. I'm looking forward to my next weekend campout. Hey, can you come up here tomorrow night for the open mic at Amped Up?

"Yeah, I think I will. It'll be something different. Give me some directions."

Bristol and Bud made their arrangements, and then talked for an hour about country music, their horses, and trails they had ridden. Suddenly Bristol said, "Gotta go," and hung up when she heard the back door open.

"You're not done, are you?" she asked Ric. "It hasn't been long enough."

"No, I'm not done. It's hot! I came in for some ice water. I thought you were going to bring me some?"

"I got busy. You've got two feet. Your salad's in the refrigerator." Bristol walked into the living room fantasizing about the next night singing with Bud.

****

Friday nights at the Amped Up were much busier than Wednesday nights. Bristol went there straight from work to grab a table for herself and Bud. She had asked the women she worked with to join her, but all of them declined.

Before leaving the office, Bristol had refreshed her makeup. She wore a low-cut, powder-blue blouse, black slacks, and sandals with gold trim. She wrapped a white cardigan around her shoulders, tying the empty sleeves in front. Her gold earrings had sapphires that sparkled even in the dim lighting.

The gum-chewing waitress in a skin-tight, leather miniskirt, and a blouse that showed as much cleavage as Bristol's, asked for her order. "I'll have a steak sandwich, no onions, a side of fries, and a beer."

Bristol glanced around as she ate her sandwich, hoping to see Bud come in early. She hoped he would be here in time to sing. People were beginning to gather for the open mic. Ernie the emcee laid his clipboard on the side of the stage for musicians to sign up. Bristol did not want to be first, and Bud might not arrive in time for the beginning, so she finished her supper and waited. She did not want to sign up too far down the list, though, because if there was time, Ernie would start calling the singers back to the stage from the top of the list again. She wanted to be sure she and Bud would have a chance to sing together a second time.

Time dragged by for Bristol as she checked her watch

frequently and watched the door for Bud. Maybe he wasn't going to show up.

Ernie hopped up on stage to welcome the audience and the musicians. "Make sure that you're on the signup sheet if you want to perform," he told them. "We'll start in about five minutes."

Bristol decided to sign them up. She could always cancel if Bud did not show.

Just as she returned to her seat, Bud walked in, carrying his guitar. He looked around the crowded room for Bristol.

Bristol stood and waved him over. "Hey, Bud, you made it!"

"It seems I did."

"I signed us up. It's going to start in a couple of minutes." Bristol smoothed her spiked hair. We're number fourteen. Sit down." Bristol and Bud sat on the same side of the table so that they could both see the stage.

They chatted a few minutes until the music began. Five people had sung their songs before the waitress made it over for Bud's order. "I'll have a beer, same as hers, and bring her another one."

The sixth musician was the beautiful woman from the other night with long, black hair who sang another blues ballad. She was followed by a harmonica player whose blues rifts brought loud applause. Two more musicians played instrumentals, and then a vocalist sang a country song while strumming chords on his Martin guitar.

When a folk singer went to the mic, Bristol turned to Bud. "Two more after her, then it's our turn," she told him. "Are you tuned up?"

"Yeah, I tuned in the other room before coming back here."

The next two performers sang country songs. Bristol thought about joining them on the stage, but she did not want to leave Bud sitting there by himself. She sang along from her seat to the annoyance of those around her and to Bud's amusement.

"Here we go," she said to Bud as Ernie called their names. Bud carried his guitar in one hand, and with his other hand he helped Bristol up the three steps to the stage.

They sang "Tumbling Tumble Weeds" as they had agreed on the phone. The crowd gave them polite applause. Bristol hoped that they would have time for a second or third song, but several other musicians had signed up after she had.

It turned out that they did have a chance to sing one more time. When they finished that song, Bud put his guitar away and walked Bristol to her car. He slid into the front seat beside her. They sat there talking for forty minutes about the open mic and about their horses before Bud said he needed to drive back to Lisbon.

****

Bristol picked up her cell phone to brag. "Hi, Nancy. I went to the Amped Up last night and Bud was there! Remember him? We met him at Beaver Creek?"

"Yes, Bristol," Nancy sighed, tired from caring for her mother and tired of Bristol. "I remember. How did he happen to drive all the way up here?"

"Oh, I invited him up to sing at the Amped Up and he came. We sang so well together at the campground, I thought it would be fun to do it again at the open mic. We got so much applause! People just loved us," she gushed.

"That's nice," Nancy said, wondering if it were true.

"I had a really great time except for the bozos who kept looking down my blouse. You'd think they never saw cleavage before."

"Maybe they never saw that much on a woman that wasn't their wife or girlfriend."

"Nancy, I didn't think you were such a prude. Grow up. Hey, guess what!"

"I haven't a clue."

"Ric bought me a Martin guitar! I'm going to learn to play it. He gave me a D18 with a beautiful mahogany top. It sounds good. Well, really he bought a D1, but I had him exchange it. It was there when I got home last night."

"He sure is good to you, Bristol. What does he think about you meeting Bud?"

"Oh, he wouldn't care. So what? We're not doing anything but singing together. You sure are a prude. I have to go. I'm in the middle of cleaning house. See you at our next campout." Bristol hung up without asking Nancy how she was doing.

Ric had left the house before Bristol was out of bed. Now she hurried to finish her housework so that she could sit down with the new guitar. She wanted to work out a few chords without Ric there to hear her mistakes as she learned. She was sure she could find guitar chords online to start with, and Monday she could stop at a music store after work to pick up a book on chords.

****

Sunday morning Bristol slept until ten o'clock. It was a beautiful morning with the prediction of staying sunny and dry. Bristol decided to call Nancy. "Let's go riding! We need to work the horses before the next campout."

"Bristol, I can't. I have my hands full with my mother right now."

"Come on, Nancy. Take a break. Have your husband manage for a day."

"Believe me, Bristol, I would love to take off and ride, but I just can't."

"My gosh, Nancy, you really are no fun anymore." She hung up without saying good-bye. She called Lavern and Elise, but Lavern was not available to ride, and Elise's husband Marty told her that Elise and Jolene were already out riding.

Huh. I wonder what Bud is doing. Bristol tried to call him, but it switched into his voice mail. She hung up without leaving a message. It was already close to eleven o'clock, and it would take her two and half hours to get ready, hitch up, and drive to Beaver Creek. Maybe she would just stay home and try to learn the basic guitar chords she had printed out yesterday.

Bristol wondered absently where Ric was as she took the Martin out of the case and tried to tune it. She could tell that she was going to have to buy one of those digital tuners.

After an hour of trying to form chords, she put the guitar away. This was harder than it looked. Her fingers did not want to stretch that way, and her fingertips were sore from pressing the strings. She could now make three of the chords, but she could not make chord changes fast enough to play them in a song.

Bristol looked out the window. She did not see Ric. She took out her cell phone and tried calling Bud again. This time he answered.

"What are you doing?" she asked him.

"I just got back from riding. I went out early this morning. How about you? When are you coming back for another weekend at Beaver Creek?"

"Soon, Bud. Anytime you want. I have vacation days coming. Let's schedule something. In fact, what are you doing the rest of today? We could meet somewhere and I could show you my new guitar. We could practice some songs together. Then we could sing something new at the open mic. Want to come up here for it Friday?"

They made plans to meet in two hours. Bristol dressed in new blue jeans that were a little tight, and a short-sleeved, low-cut blouse that was long enough to cover some of her too-round middle. She carefully applied makeup and added silver earrings.

She grabbed the guitar and left the house without leaving a note for Ric.

****

Mid-morning on Monday, Bristol walked into the office of Larry Brown, her boss. "How about going out to lunch today, Larry? Let's go to Dontino's. I'm hungry for Italian." She made herself comfortable in the chair across from his big desk.

Larry adjusted his burgundy silk tie. He looked at the stack of reports sitting on his desk. "I don't know, Bristol. I have a lot going on. This is the first of the month with all of last month's reports going out."

"Oh, come on, boss. You need to take it easy. You don't want to die of stress. The work will still be here after you take a break. Is there anything I can do for you? I could figure out a way to work it into my busy schedule." Bristol leaned forward and squeezed her arms together to gain the maximum cleavage into the deep V neck of her red blouse.

"Larry? How about we leave at twelve-thirty?" Bristol was thinking that the rest of the office staff would already be at lunch and they would not see her leave with the boss. She did not want them to think that she was brown-nosing the boss. "That will give us both more time to finish some work and we can relax better. Then when we come back, we can hit it hard again. I'll stay over a couple of hours tonight. OK?"

Larry's blue eyes left the cleavage and looked at Bristol's face. "All right. We can make it a working lunch. You can update me about the office staff."

"Yes, Sir." Bristol stood and saluted, turned and walked out of the office with a sly grin. *Men are so easy,* she thought.

****

The working lunch was just that with Bristol asking for advanced information on any of the company's plans for the future, complaining about the certified public accountants in the office, taking credit for an idea proposed to her by one of them, and bragging about her own work.

Larry had driven Bristol to Dontino's while the rest of the staff was already on their lunch hour. When they returned to the office, Bristol told Larry that she needed something from her car and that she would be upstairs in a few minutes. After giving Larry time to enter the office without her in tow, she entered the building, hoping that no one would notice or put her together with Larry.

As Bristol sauntered through the common area toward her office, she heard Tracie whisper to two of the other women, "Look at that. I'll bet you where she's been – out with the boss." The three of them snickered.

Bristol turned and snapped, "Mind your own business. You have work to do. You're just showing that you're jealous! Anyway, you have no idea where I've been. You're playing stupid, and it looks like you're winning!" She stormed into her office and slammed the door.

At the end of the day, the office staff had cleared out by ten after five. When Bristol heard the boss close his office door, she stepped into the common room and went to the copier with a stack of papers. "Have a good night, Larry, and thanks again for the lunch," she told him as he was leaving.

"That's all right, Bristol. Don't stay too late, now. See you in the morning."

"Oh, I'll only be a couple of hours. You have a good night, too."

Bristol waited until Larry walked out of the door, then she took the stack of papers back to her office, laid them on her desk, and walked to the window overlooking the parking lot. While waiting for Larry to reach his car, she thought, *I don't understand why people don't like me. I'm just as good as those college grads, even better. None of them can play the game like I can. They'll be sorry for not supporting me.* As soon as she saw Larry drive out of the parking lot, she left for home.

CHAPTER 4
LAVERN

It was a Saturday early in June. Lavern woke up early. She wished it was a work day for her husband Charlie. Lavern worked for the local school system and summer break had just begun, but Charlie worked year-round. Weekends seemed to bring trouble with Charlie. She quickly and quietly slipped out of bed before Charlie would wake up, reach for her, and tell her, "Let's make a baby." That was not a turn-on for Lavern. No, it was not even close to romantic.

She threw a load of laundry into the machine on her way to the bathroom. She hoped to complete her housework by noon and drive to the boarding stable where she kept her horse Lacy. She planned to groom her and maybe even ride her for a couple of hours.

After her shower, she put the coffee on to brew and started breakfast. The smell of frying bacon would wake Charlie. She would wait until he was ready to eat before cooking the eggs. The toast popped up, and Charlie walked into the kitchen.

"Good morning, Beautiful," he nuzzled her neck. "I like your hair pulled back like this. It shows off your neck." He blew a wet raspberry under her brown pony tail.

With her wrist, Lavern wiped at the wet spot on her neck as Charlie turned to sit at the kitchen table. She pulled the toast from the toaster, but before she could butter it, Charlie demanded, "Bring me a cup of coffee, Darlin'."

"Charlie, I need to butter the toast while it's hot. I'll get it for you in a minute."

In a flash, Charlie was on his feet grabbing the same neck he had just nuzzled, this time in a not-so-gentle squeeze. "Darlin', when your man asks you for a simple cup of coffee, you bring it to him and right then. Do you understand?" His normal, soft drawl was gone. His tone was rough, a near growl.

Lavern swallowed her fear and said in a cheerful voice, "Of course, Charlie. You sit down, and I'll get it for you. It just finished brewing." She added the milk and sugar the way Charlie liked it and set the mug in front of him.

She started frying the eggs and pushed the toast back down to warm. There was no sense in giving Charlie something to be upset about if she could help it. Too often of late, it seemed that she could not help it. She drained the bacon, then carefully fried the eggs over easy so that the whites were cooked and the yellow was still a little runny. She knew that they turned out exactly the way he liked them, but when they began eating, he complained.

"Now, when are you going to learn how to cook like a real wife?" he drawled. "This bacon is greasy, and the eggs aren't right." He tapped the edge of his plate with his fork.

Lavern was not going to fall for asking him what was wrong with the eggs. She remembered the counselor telling her that Charlie's unwarranted criticisms were only for the purpose of controlling her. The counselor had told her to try to acknowledge the criticism as though it were reasonable, but not to become involved in an argument about it.

"I'll try to do better for you next time, Charlie," she said in an even voice.

"See that you do." Charlie seemed satisfied. There was no more conversation until they had finished eating when he said, "Today we're going to take the motorcycle out for a spin. Clean up this mess and be ready to ride in twenty minutes. I'm going to read the paper."

Lavern was just finishing her coffee. She set down the cup and looked at Charlie. She used to think he was handsome, but since their marriage when he began trying to control her, she no longer thought he was handsome.

"Charlie, I was going to do laundry and clean house this morning, and I would like to go to the barn to see Lacy this afternoon. I haven't been out there all week." Lavern wiped her lips with her napkin.

"Well, *I* say we're going for a bike ride! So what do you say to that?" Charlie pounded the table once with his fist for emphasis.

"Charlie, I can change my plans for you and do the housework tomorrow, even though I hate doing that on a Sunday. Could you work in a trip to the barn for me while we're out on the bike? Would it matter where we ride?" Lavern was pleading. She wondered how Bristol would handle this. *In the first place, Charlie would never be able to intimidate Bristol,* she thought. *Geez, Bristol might even intimidate Charlie!*

"Yeah, sure, since you ask all sweet like that. I'll give you a half hour at the barn. Then we'll ride up around the Punderson

Lake area and wherever the bike takes us." Charlie went outside for the morning paper without waiting for a reply from Lavern.

There goes my ride on Lacy, Lavern thought. *At least I'll get to see her.* Lavern put the clothes from the washer into the dryer and hurried to clean up the kitchen. She wanted to be ready to go in twenty minutes whether Charlie was ready or not.

Twenty minutes later, Lavern was ready. Charlie was still reading the paper. Lavern sat down in the living room across from him. Charlie kept reading.

"I'm ready if you want to go," she told him.

"When I'm done with the paper."

It was a half hour later when Charlie folded the paper, stood up, and stretched. "Ok, let's get going. It's getting late. I want a full day on the bike."

He backed the red Honda out of the garage while Lavern put on her helmet. Charlie did not ride with a helmet. He wore leather pants and a sleeveless leather vest. Lavern had on blue jeans and a leather halter top that Charlie insisted she wear when riding the bike. They put their leather jackets in the storage compartment of the bike and started their trip.

When Charlie roared past the road that would take them to Buckeye Farm where Lacy was boarded, Lavern tapped him on his back. "We missed the turn for the barn," she shouted into his ear over the noise of the engine.

"No, I didn't. We're not going there. We got too late a start," Charlie shouted back.

Lavern was disappointed, but she knew better than to argue with Charlie. She would never win an argument with him, and it would just anger him if she tried. She determined to make the best of it and enjoy the bike ride. She just wished that he would be more thoughtful of her.

They continued up Route 44 into Shalersville Township, past farms with corn, hay and soy bean fields, and stands of woods. They crossed over the Ohio Turnpike. Lavern was grateful that Charlie did not turn left there to enter the turnpike. The speed limit was 70, and she knew Charlie would run the bike over the limit. It scared her.

After a few hills, Charlie slowed to 25 to ease through the town of Mantua. On the other side, they crossed the Cuyahoga River and sped through more farmland. Shortly after crossing Route 82, Charlie turned left into the driveway of a Harley Davidson dealership and stopped.

"Come on, we're going in," he told Lavern after backing his Honda into a parking space and climbing off.

"Why? What do you want in a Harley store?" she asked him.

"Don't question me," Charlie snapped. He grabbed Lavern's arm as she was climbing off the bike and jerked her the rest of the way off. He marched her into the store, squeezing her arm tightly.

Charlie found a salesman who was willing to spend all the time Charlie needed to discuss the various Harley models, features and benefits, and pricing. The fellow even talked to his sales manager so he could give Charlie a trade-in value on his Honda. Lavern stayed silent at Charlie's side.

It was close to two hours when Charlie was satisfied and they left the store.

"Charlie, we can't afford any of those Harleys now. Aren't you happy with this bike?" Lavern asked him while putting on her helmet.

"Well, we could afford it if you sold that stupid horse of yours. You have to pay monthly board on it, and then there's the blacksmith and sometimes vet bills. You sell it, and we can easy buy a Harley." Charlie climbed on the Honda, lifted the kick stand, and rocked the bike back and forth under him feeling the balance.

A cold chill gripped Lavern around her heart. She loved Lacy and she loved riding her. She decided not to begin an argument with Charlie at this time, and swung on behind him without responding.

Charlie continued north on Route 44. Lavern saw a sign for alpacas, pounded Charlie's right shoulder, and pointed. "Let's stop and look at them," she shouted.

Charlie shook his head no, and kept going. They entered Geauga County. The farms and a few housing developments sped by. They came to LaDue Public Hunting and Fishing area with a lake and woodlands. Charlie sped up and leaned into the curves, and then had to pull back when he caught up to traffic going the speed limit. Lavern knew that would make him angry, but she felt safer going more slowly. She hoped that they would not have a collision with a deer. They saw water and she did not know whether it was still LaDue or part of Punderson Lake.

When they came into the small town of Newbury, Charlie turned left onto route 87 and took them past the Punderson area with its lakes and woods. They were again traveling through farms and woodlands and now beautiful rock formations rose from the roadside. Lavern saw a sign for the West Woods Nature Center. She again pounded Charlie's shoulder and pointed. "Let's stop and check it out," she shouted. Again, he shook his head no and kept going.

They crossed Silver Creek and the Chagrin River, and passed by woods and many horse properties with beautiful large homes and barns. The road curved right and followed the river to the Polo Fields in Moreland Hills. They crossed Route 91 and hit the city traffic of Pepper Pike. Charlie turned south on I-271 and opened up the bike even though it was fairly heavy traffic. Lavern held on tight.

Finally he exited onto Route 303 and drove west into the small town of Peninsula in the Cuyahoga Valley National Park. Next to the Tow Path trail for hikers and bicyclists was a Winking Lizard Tavern. Charlie pulled in, and they went inside to eat.

Charlie ordered a hamburger, fries, and beer. Lavern ordered a salad and Pepsi. When the drinks arrived, Charlie took a few sips of his beer and called the waitress over. "This isn't cold enough," he told her.

"I'm sorry, Sir. I'll bring you another, or would you like something else?" She looked tired.

"Just bring me a colder one," Charlie told her and got up to use the restroom.

Lavern looked up at him. "It looked cold. Wasn't it, really?"

"It was fine. I just wanted to keep them on their toes. I'll be right back," and Charlie walked off.

Lavern was embarrassed. She hoped that Charlie would not make another fuss.

He did not, and they rode the bike back east on Route 303 to Routes 14 and 44 to home.

****

Lavern's heart was racing. It felt as though it were both beating rapidly and thumping through her chest. She considered going to the emergency room, but she decided that it was stress and made an appointment with her general practitioner instead. The receptionist told her to have someone drive her in right away. Since Charlie was at work, Lavern drove herself.

She was hustled into an exam room after measuring her current weight. The nurse took her blood pressure and temperature, and updated her information. "The doctor will be right in."

Lavern only waited five minutes before the doctor knocked and entered. "So, what have we here? Are you having chest pains?"

"Well, no, not really. My heart was racing, and it was pounding like it would come out of my chest, but it quit. I seem to be back to normal now, but it scared me."

The doctor looked over her chart. "Your blood pressure, pulse, and temperature are normal now. Has this happened to you before?"

"No, this is the first time, and I hope it's the last."

"Let me listen." The doctor used his stethoscope and had Lavern take deep breaths. "Umm. Your heart and lungs both sound good. Let's get an EKG. I'll send in the nurse." With that, the doctor was gone.

The nurse came back in and told Lavern to take off all of her clothes from the waist up and put on the gown with the opening in the front. "I'll be back in a few," she said as she left.

When the nurse returned, she hooked Lavern up to the EKG machine. When the test was over, she told Lavern to dress and the doctor would be back in.

Lavern had to wait ten minutes before the doctor came back. "The EKG shows no abnormality. We can wait to see if this event happens again, or I can set you up with a twenty-four hour heart monitor to try to catch another episode."

"I don't know." Thinking of her troubles with Charlie, she said, "Maybe it won't happen again. I've been under a lot of stress recently. Could this be caused by stress?"

"It very well could be. Since your EKG is normal, we could wait and see whether you have another episode. If you do, be sure to call me right away. I would like to have you wear the heart monitor, so that I can see what is happening." The doctor wrote on her chart. "Tell you what, come back in two weeks and let me know how it goes." With that, the doctor left the room.

Lavern left without making an appointment telling herself that this was just stress. She drove to the barn to spend a relaxing hour with Lacy before driving home to prepare a nice dinner for Charlie.

Charlie usually came home from work around five-thirty. Sometimes he stopped at a local bar and came home later. He never called her to tell her that he would be late, but he expected a hot meal to be on the table whenever he did come in the door. Tonight was their six-thirty appointment with the marriage counselor, so she expected him home on time.

At six-thirty, Lavern called the counselor to explain that Charlie had not yet come home and to apologize for missing the appointment. Charlie walked in the door just after seven. Lavern met him at the door. "Where have you been? We missed the counseling appointment. Did you forget?"

"That's no way to greet your husband. You should be making nice and giving me a kiss." Charlie grabbed Lavern and kissed her hard on her lips. "Supper better be on the table. I'm hungry."

"Yes, it's ready." Lavern dashed to the kitchen to lift the food from the pan keeping it warm. She quickly set it on the table while Charlie used the bathroom.

They sat at the table together. Charlie always expected Lavern to wait to eat with him even when he was late.

"Pass the mashed potatoes. They better be real and not made from a box."

Lavern was about to tell him about the episode with her heart when Charlie began to complain about the marriage counselor.

"So," he continued, "I think it's a waste of time and you can cancel the rest of our appointments. I'm not going back."

Lavern was disappointed. Counseling had been her only hope of saving her marriage, but she was afraid to argue with Charlie. They continued to eat in silence while she processed the idea of her marriage failing.

Charlie finished eating and asked, "What's for dessert? Did you bake that apple pie I asked you to make? I don't want any store bought substitute. My mother's pie was always the best. Bring it on, woman."

Lavern cleared the table and brought in her freshly-baked pie and more coffee. She felt like an under-appreciated slave instead of like a beloved wife. She felt like throwing the pie in Charlie's face, but she sat down and calmly served him.

Charlie finished his pie and coffee, threw down his napkin, and jumped up from the table. "I'm going outside to work on the bike."

When Lavern had the kitchen cleaned up, Charlie was still outside. She went to bed.

In the morning Lavern overslept and she had to hurry to make Charlie's breakfast and pack his lunch in time for him to leave for work. In her rush, she did not mention the event with her heart. There had been no other episodes.

Her day was busy with vacuuming, dusting, and grocery shopping. She had to hurry to make dinner on time. Maybe she would have a chance to ride Lacy tomorrow.

Dinner was on the table by five-thirty when Charlie walked in the door. She greeted him with a kiss that was not heart-felt.

"Well, Darlin', that's the way a man wants to come home, to a hot meal and a hot wife. Let's eat first, then let's go upstairs and make a baby."

****

As bad as he had been, Charlie was becoming even more demanding and quicker to anger. He almost hit Lavern the previous night when the potatoes she was boiling spilled over onto the stove top. Nothing was ever good enough, clean enough, fast enough. She knew that staying would mean poor health, broken bones, and a miserable life, so Lavern devised a plan. She needed to make a clean break from Charlie and not give him an opportunity to hurt her when he found out that she was leaving.

They did not own their home. They rented an apartment and

the lease was in his name. The furniture was his from before they married. She could easily move out with just her clothes and several boxes of personal items. She needed a place to live, and then she could begin moving her belongings a couple of boxes at a time so that Charlie would not notice.

They had joint bank accounts. There were only twelve hundred dollars in savings and around eight hundred in checking. Their only bills were rent, utilities, cell phone, his car payment, and his motorcycle payment. She had no problem with leaving him with those bills since he was the one who would reap the benefits. She would stop using her cell phone that was on their family plan and buy a new phone with an account in her own name. She would continue to pay her horse board. She needed to withdraw half of the money from each bank account on the day she would leave. She wanted to be fair to Charlie, even though she knew he would never be fair with her.

With Charlie's anger escalating, she was afraid that he was going to hurt her the next time that he blew up. Because that might happen before she could find an apartment, she needed to be prepared for a fast getaway. On her last trip to the grocery store, Lavern had a spare set of car and house keys made. She put the keys in a duffle bag with fifty dollars cash that she had been saving. She added underwear, two pairs of jeans, three T shirts, a photo album with pictures of her deceased parents, and her birth certificate, social security card, and teaching certificate. If she had to flee from Charlie in a hurry with nothing else from here, she would have the most important items.

She packed some jewelry and some dress clothes that she would not be wearing this summer into a cardboard box and taped it shut.

She called Nancy. "Hey, Nancy, could I come by and drop

something off for you to keep for me? I need to talk to you, too."

Nancy told her that she would be home and to come over.

Lavern left the box in the car and carried the duffle bag into Nancy's house. Nancy's mother was dressing a lavender stuffed puppy in doll clothes that Nancy had bought her at a garage sale. Nancy and Lavern sat in the kitchen where Nancy could keep an eye on her mother and they could talk.

"What's up?" Nancy asked, eyeing the duffle bag suspiciously.

"I'm leaving Charlie."

"Oh, Honey. I knew you were going to have to some day. I'm so sorry." Nancy gave Lavern a hug.

"No, no, it's OK. I'm all right about it. Actually, I'm beginning to feel a sense of freedom and I know that I'll have more peace when it's done."

"Are you asking to stay here? Is that all you brought with you?"

"No, I haven't left yet. I just need you to keep this bag for me until I have a place of my own. It has stuff I'll need if I have to leave in a hurry before I'm ready. But, could I stay here if I have to leave before I find an apartment?"

"I can keep your bag, but you know I don't have room for you to stay. You would be welcome to my couch for a couple of days, but with Mom here ..."

"I know. I understand. Thanks for this. It has the spare sets of my car keys, truck keys, and trailer keys in it, plus some clothes and papers. I'm going to box up more clothes and some other things and hide them in my horse trailer. Then on my escape day I can box up the last bit of my stuff and go while Charlie's at work. I sure hope he doesn't figure it out until I'm gone." Lavern twisted a strand of her hair.

"Honey, good luck to you. You know I support you. I'll do what I can for you, and I'll be praying for both you and Charlie. He has an emotional sickness, but I'm glad you're leaving before he hurts you. Will you be able to go on our next campout?"

"I'm counting on it. I need it!" Lavern thought about telling Nancy about her racing, hard-beating heart, but decided not to worry her. Certainly it was due to stress.

Lavern walked into the living room to speak with Nancy's mother. "Hello, Mary. How are you today?"

Mary did not answer. Lavern tried again, "What do you have here? It's a pretty puppy."

Mary squealed, "It's mine! Leave it alone! It's mine!" and hid the stuffed dog behind her back. "No, no, no, it's mine! You can't have it!"

Lavern backed up. "Sorry. I'm sorry. It's yours, all yours, Mary."

"I'm sorry, Lavern," Nancy apologized for her mother. "She was never like this before. It's the disease. Nobody can touch that dog without her having a fit."

The two women hugged, and Nancy walked Lavern to the door. "I hope I'm not disappointing you, Nancy, because I'm leaving my husband. I know you go to church, so I figure you don't believe in divorce."

"No, no, I already told you that I'm glad you won't be there for him to hurt you. An abuser is dangerous. You be careful."

Lavern drove to Buckeye Farm and carried the cardboard box of clothes to her horse trailer. She stored the box in the third stall of the trailer next to her camping gear, and locked the trailer again. *That's one box,* she thought. Tomorrow she would pack two or three more boxes of clothes she would not soon need, and bring them out here. She would also open a new account in her name only at a different bank. The next day she would go to the school administration building to fill out the paper work to change her direct deposit paycheck to the new account. Once that was done, she would have to be gone and out of Charlie's reach before her next paycheck was due.

Lavern went into the pasture for her horse. She led Lacy to the hitching rail and spent a soothing hour grooming her.

****

Lavern left her lawyer's office scared but happy. She was worried about Charlie's reaction to her filing for divorce, but she was relieved and happy to have it underway. She still had not found a suitable apartment, but she had called Elise to explain her situation and to ask if she could stay with her temporarily. Elise had talked it over with her husband, and they had agreed.

Tomorrow would be her last day with Charlie. She would see him off to work in the morning, hurriedly pack her last boxes of belongings, withdraw half of the money from their bank accounts, deposit it in her new checking account at the other bank, buy a new cell phone, call her friends with her new number, and drive out to the farm to store the last of the boxes in the horse trailer. She would spend the rest of the day looking for an apartment before going to Elise's. She hated to impose on Elise and her family, but she was glad not to have to rush into taking just any apartment. She wanted to find her new place and unload these boxes from the trailer before the next campout. The boxes were making it crowded in the trailer.

The day went as planned. Slade Meyers, the tall, lean, tanned, farm owner, helped Lavern to unload the boxes from her car and store them in her horse trailer. Lavern explained that she was leaving Charlie with divorce papers soon to be served.

"Slade, I'm really worried about Charlie's need for control and how mean and angry he can be. Please watch out for Lacy and my rig, OK?"

"Miss Lavern, you have enough to worry about. Don't be worrying about your mare and rig. I'll make sure nothin' happens to them."

****

When Charlie came home from work the next day, he was surprised that not only was dinner not ready, but Lavern was not in the apartment.

She's going to get it! Just the other night when he had to wait five minutes for dinner, he talked to her about how she had her freedom all day while he worked, and how the least she could do was to have his dinner ready for him the moment he came through the door. His anger began to build. It turned into a rage when he found her note on his pillow telling him that she had left him and that divorce papers would be coming. He did not bother to take the time to change from his good work clothes. He slammed the door and ran to the garage.

Charlie squealed out of the drive on his motorcycle, his

necktie blowing in the wind. He was furious. *How dare she! I won't let her go! I'll show her!* He headed toward the stable where Lacy was boarded and the truck and trailer were kept. *I'll take that horse she loves more than me to the sale barn for the meat buyers.*

The back tire on the Honda slid on the gravel as it made the turn into the Buckeye Farm driveway. Charlie kept the bike upright and slammed it to a stop next to the long, one story horse barn. He hoped the horse was in the stall and not in the pasture where he would have to catch it. It came to Lavern, but not to him.

Lacy was indeed in the middle of the three-acre pasture. Charlie decided to hitch the truck to the trailer first, and then he would go after the horse. Charlie used the set of truck and trailer keys that he carried on his own key ring. Lavern had been unable to take them without him realizing they were missing. He was backing up the Dodge Ram when Slade, in denim overalls and a straw hat, came up to the open window of the truck.

"Going somewhere?" Slade asked him, leaning his long frame on the edge of the open truck window.

"Oh, yeah, I sure am," Charlie said with a smirk.

"You aim on taking the horse?" Slade spit a wade of chew.

"Yup, I do, and it won't be back, so you can rent out that stall space to someone else."

Slade tipped back his straw hat, spit another wad of chew, and said, "Uh, huh." He pushed off from the truck and walked away toward the house.

Charlie hitched the gooseneck to the truck and pulled the rig forward enough to open the back trailer doors and to pull down the ramp ready to load the horse. He did not notice the boxes stacked in the last two stalls of the trailer.

He went into the barn. There was no halter or lead rope hanging in front of Lacy's stall, so he grabbed a nylon halter with a cotton lead from the hook next to another stall. Hiding the halter and lead behind his back, he went into the pasture to catch the horse. Three horses grazing closest to him moved off together. He ignored them and went straight toward Lacy who looked up from her grazing to watch him. When he was close, she turned and trotted away.

"Don't piss me off!" he yelled at the horse and approached it again. Two teenage girls in short shorts, halter tops, and cowboy boots, grooming their horses at a hitching rail outside the barn, stopped what they were doing to watch him. "Such a dude!" one said to the other. "We have to watch this. It should be fun."

After twenty frustrating minutes of trying to catch a horse that did not want to be caught, stepping in horse manure with his tasseled loafers, and getting dust on his Dockers, one of the girls, the blond with a pony tail, offered to help Charlie.

Pony Tail took the halter and lead from Charlie. She nonchalantly walked diagonally toward Lacy in an arc instead of approaching her directly. She did not look at the horse. Her path would take her past the horse, but when she was nearly past and only two feet from the mare, she turned toward her and quickly put the lead around Lacy's neck. She held the lead close around the mare's neck with one hand while she slipped the halter over Lacy's head with her other hand. Pony Tail clipped the lead onto the halter and offered it to Charlie.

She made catching the horse look so easy that Charlie became angrier. He grabbed the lead rope and stalked off leading Lacy out of the pasture, through the barn, and outside. Scowling, he turned the corner and headed for the truck and trailer.

Slade, who had been leaning against the front of the Dodge, unfolded his long legs and uncradled a Browning shotgun he had been holding against his chest. He pointed the gun at Charlie.

"Whoa, now. What are you doing?" Charlie asked him in surprise. He stopped short and Lacy, following him, bumped into his shoulder, knocking him forward two steps.

"Just waitin' on the sheriff," Slade answered, still pointing the gun at Charlie. "He ought to be here right about now, so we shouldn't have much of a wait. I called him right after I talked to you. You ain't takin' that horse anywhere, or this truck and trailer either, if I have anything to do with it. Miss Lavern told me to watch out for you, that you might try something with her rig and her horse.

"Now you just hold on," Charlie sputtered, aghast. "This is my horse as much as hers. She's my wife, so ..."

"Save it for the sheriff. Here he comes now." Slade gestured toward the driveway with his head.

The sheriff's deputy had been rolling with no lights and no siren, but now, seeing Slade with the shotgun pointed at Charlie, he turned on his lights and gave one burst of the siren. *Ya have to let them know the law is here,* he thought. *Sometimes it saves trouble.*

"Howdy. Deputy Dixon," he introduced himself. "You Slade Meyers, the one who made the call?"

"Yes, sir, I am." Slade lowered the gun and tipped his hat. "This polecat is Charlie Smith. He's the one tryin' to steal this here horse and rig."

"That right? Well, what do you have to say? It does look like you're makin' ready to leave with this horse."

Charlie was too stunned to speak for a moment. In his anger he had not anticipated anything like this. Lacy nudged his shoulder from behind as though telling him to speak up. He slapped at the horse's face. Lacy threw her head high and backed up a step. Her action pulled enough lead rope loose to be able to lower her head and graze.

"Well?" Deputy Dixon asked him.

"This is my horse. Mine and my wife's. I'm taking it somewhere else. I have every right."

"That depends," the deputy said thoughtfully, wiping the sweat from his brow, his hat in his other hand. "Do you have papers on this horse? Is it registered? How about a bill of sale? I want to see something with your name on it as owner." He put his hat back on his head.

"I don't know. I mean yes, it's a registered Tennessee Walker, but the papers would be back at the house somewhere. But Slade here knows it's my horse." Slade frowned at him and Charlie added, "Mine and my wife's."

Slade reached into his back pocket and produced a document for the deputy. "Will this help? It's the boarding agreement signed by his wife, Lavern. I believe this is her mare. She lists herself as the owner and doesn't mention the husband here."

"Let me have a look see." The deputy reached for the papers. "Yeah, he's right," the deputy told Charlie after reading them over. "Looks like it's her horse to me. Maybe you should just go put that...," the deputy took a quick look under the horse's belly, "... mare back in the barn."

"Well she just didn't think to add my name at the time.

Maybe we weren't married yet."

"Oh, ho!" The deputy slapped his thigh. "So you weren't married when your now wife bought this horse, huh? I reckon your name's not on any paperwork showing ownership, then. That makes me wonder about this here truck and trailer. You have the registrations for them?"

Charlie was on no safer ground here. "Sure. They should be in the glove box." He dropped the lead rope and moved toward the truck.

The deputy picked up the rope, handed it to Slade, and told Charlie, "You just hold on here, Son. Let me check it out." Deputy Dixon did not want Charlie to pull out a gun. After a quick look in the glove box for a gun, he told Charlie it was all right to look for the registration papers. "You can put away that horse," he told Slade, "and put away the shotgun while you're at it."

"Yes, Sir," Slade agreed, and walked Lacy into the pasture.

"Well? Any papers?"

Charlie was rifling through the glove box, but he did not pull out the registration papers. He knew the truck and trailer were in Lavern's name. "I know this truck's in my name," he lied. "I bought it for her to pull the trailer. She had an old beater when I met her and I wanted her to be safe."

"Now, Son, you know I can run the plates. I'm not so sure you want me to do that. How about you just run along without making a problem, hear? I don't want any trouble."

Charlie stalked off and climbed on his bike. The deputy warned him, "Don't you be coming around here making more trouble. I understand from Mr. Meyers that your wife is divorcing you. You let the lawyers and the court handle who ends up with what."

Slade was leaning against the side of the barn. "Thanks, Deputy Dixon. I appreciate your coming out and handling this. Miss Lavern sure does love her horse. Truth to tell, I think divorcing that jerk will do her a world of good. Now she'll get to spend more time with that mare again, and maybe she'll get back to being the confident gal I knew when she first started boarding here, before she got married."

The deputy nodded. "Now, don't go shooting anyone, but don't let him remove that rig without registration papers in his name. Same for the horse. You done right to call me. Call again if you need any help. I'd rather stop a problem before it starts."

The two men shook hands and Deputy Dixon drove off. Slade spit tobacco juice and went inside to call Lavern on her new cell phone to let her know what Charlie had tried. He chuckled to himself. *Miss Lavern's going to think I'm pretty cool for an eighty-two year old man.*

Slade's call to tell her about Charlie scared Lavern. She had known Charlie would be angry, but now she realized that he was in a rage. Slade suggested that she should not go anywhere that Charlie might know to look for her, and not to tell anyone where she was going. That probably left Elise's place out. If Charlie was going to hunt for her, he would check with each of her friends.

Suddenly she had an idea. She thanked Slade, closed her cell phone, and turned to the apartment manager who was showing her a unit in his complex of four buildings. "I'll take it, if I can move in today," she told him. It was not exactly what she was looking for, but it was freshly painted and clean and it was just a ten minute drive from the school where she taught. Most important to her was that the door into the building was always locked. A key to both the building and to the apartment would be needed.

The friends were going on their June campout next weekend. Lavern had requested that they go to Harrison State Forest in order to be farther away from Charlie in a place they had never been so that Charlie would not think to look for her there. Why not go early, like right now? That would keep her, Lacy, and the rig out of Charlie's reach. Everything she owned was now in the horse trailer anyway. She could drive it here, unload into the apartment, and take off for Harrison. Charlie would never find her all summer until she returned to the school in the fall.

"We can start the paperwork today, but I have to check your references and credit, and look for any criminal record," the manager told her.

"Look, I'm really in a hurry. I'm going on vacation until the end of August and I need a place to put all my stuff. There's no furniture, just boxes. How about if you call my references now, I pay you for two months in advance, and you let me store my stuff here until the end of August. I won't move in until like, maybe, August 15. Honestly, you won't find anything you don't like in my credit or criminal reports, and if you did, you can issue me an eviction notice before I even really move in. Come on." Lavern could see no problem with her plan for herself or for the apartment manager.

He thought it over for a minute, and then said, "OK, come with me to the office. I'll make your reference calls."

"Thanks, oh, thanks. I appreciate it. I want to leave today. How about I go get my things then check in with you for the keys?"

They agreed on that.

On the way to the barn she stopped for groceries since she had taken no food from the apartment she had called home with Charlie. She stocked up for two weeks. She would have bought more, but the trailer would only hold so much. She would have to unhook the trailer and drive to a grocery in Cadiz, the nearest town to Harrison Forest, when she ran out of food.

At the farm, she unloaded the groceries into the living quarters of the gooseneck. She started the refrigerator and put the cold food inside. She had already emptied the water from the water system after the last trip. Now she began refilling it with fresh water. She checked the air pressure in the tires of the truck and trailer and was satisfied. She checked the oil and coolant levels in the truck. They were right on the mark.

Just as she popped the hood back down, Slade came up behind her.

"Oh, you scared me!"

"Sorry, Miss Lavern. I sure didn't mean to. Looks like you're going to take off. I thought you weren't going camping until Friday."

"That was the plan, but I'm moving it up. I'm getting out of Dodge while it's too hot in this town." Lavern wiped her hands on a paper towel.

"Good thinkin' Miss Lavern. I'm not gonna ask you where you're goin', but I am gonna ask you to take this here pistol. Just in case. Do you know how to use it?"

"Ah, Slade, thank you. You are a gem. No, I don't know about shooting guns and I don't want to learn. Look, though. I'm carrying pepper spray." Lavern took the small canister from her back jeans pocket.

"Missy, that's just fine if you know which way the wind's blowing when you go to use it. Is it fresh? They don't last forever." Slade spit tobacco.

"Yeah, Slade, I bought it today." Lavern put it back in her pocket. "I'm going to load hay and grain, get Lacy, and I'm ready to roll. Thank you."

"I'll help you with those hay bales. Let's get you out of here before that jerk comes back lookin' for you. I'd hate to have to shoot him."

They filled the second stall of the trailer with as many hay bales as they could fit in front of her boxes, and added a full sack of grain. She now had boxes in two of the stalls, and in the living quarters. She wished she could have unloaded the boxes before today to have room for more hay. She would have to unload Lacy and tie her to the trailer while she unloaded at the apartment. She hoped the manager would not be upset with the horse in front of his building for a short while.

Lavern was ready. She loaded Lacy. She climbed into the truck and kissed Slade on his cheek from her open cab window.

"Good bye, you cool old man. I love you!"

Slade beamed as he watched her drive away.

CHAPTER 5
ELISE

Jolene was still sleeping. Elise had been up since six-thirty to fix her husband's breakfast and pack his lunch. After Marty left for work at seven-thirty, Elise ate her own breakfast, then went to the barn to feed and water the two horses.

Their Tennessee Walkers, Tricked Out and Tucker, were standing by the gate. Tucker nickered a greeting. They were covered in mud where they had rolled on the wet ground.

Elise entered the barn, poured their grain into the feed tubs in the two stalls, and opened the back barn door. The horses came in and went into their own stalls. Elise latched the stall doors and Trick made contented sighs as he ate. Tucker finished first and began banging on his stall door with his hoof. He wanted back out to graze on the grass in the back pasture.

"Quit that!" Elise yelled at him. He did not stop. Elise picked up the buggy whip and shook it in front of Tuck's stall door. He showed the whites of his eyes and backed up. Elise thought it funny that the horse would respect the whip even though he had never been hurt by it.

She checked the water in the bathtub that served as a water trough in the front pasture next to the barn. The level was nearly full. She could wait until tomorrow to fill it back up. There was no need to put hay out because the horses ate grass in the warm months. The hay was for winter weather and for camping when the horses were on a picket line. She was about to turn the horses back out to pasture when she had an idea.

"Jolene," she called upstairs when she reached the house. "Get yourself out of bed and let's go riding!" There was no answer, so she climbed the stairs.

Jolene was in her room with a light summer sheet over her head. She groaned. "I don't want to get up."

"Come on, Jolene. We need to work the horses and it'll be fun. Let's go to Walborn Reservoir, or to Quail Hollow, or anywhere you want to go. I'll even drive us to Cuyahoga Valley if you want to ride there." Ohio had many state parks and some metro parks with bridle trails. Cuyahoga Valley was a national park with bridle trails. Most of these trails were built and maintained by volunteers.

Jolene stayed under the sheet and groaned again. Elise grabbed the sheet and pulled it down. "Mom, what are you doing? I want to sleep."

"Come on. You need the fresh air and exercise. Once you're up, you'll be happy to go riding. Hurry up and dress. I'll make you breakfast and pack lunches for us."

Jolene groaned again, but her feet hit the floor.

Elise went downstairs to prepare the food.

When they were ready, Elise hitched the horse trailer to the truck with Jolene guiding her. Everything they would need was already in the trailer. Lead ropes and halters hung in front of each stall in the barn. Elise haltered Tucker and led him to the trailer while Jolene haltered Tricked Out and brought him outside.

"Man, these horses are dirty!" she told her mother. "It's going to take awhile to groom them before we ride."

The horses stepped into the trailer one after the other. Elise tied their lead ropes to the trailer with horseman's knots, and Jolene closed the ramp. Elise went out the escape door, and the women climbed into the truck cab.

"Where to?" Elise asked Jolene. "Your pick."

"Let's go to Quail Hollow. It's closer than Cuyahoga Valley and it has more woods than Walborn." Jolene fastened her seat belt.

"OK. Here we go." Elise buckled up and hauled them to the state park in Hartville. They pulled onto the grass parallel to the road and unloaded the horses. The park supplied hitching posts, but they tied their horses to the side of the trailer. There was only one other horse trailer parked there. It was a rusting two-horse bumper-pull.

They used curry combs in circular motions to brush the caked mud from the horses. The mud and dust flew. When the horses were finally clean, they brushed them with soft brushes in the direction the hair grew, leaving a gleaming shine on their black hides. Tucker was standing on three legs, the fourth foot cocked. His eyes were closed. Tricked Out was also relaxed with his head as far down as the lead rope allowed. Occasionally they swished a fly with their tail.

"I don't know about you, Jolene, but I just worked up an appetite. Let's eat our sandwiches."

"OK, Mom." Jolene carried their drinks up the little hill to where the park had supplied a picnic table for the trail riders. Elise was right behind her with sandwiches, apples and hand sanitizer.

"Sorry to wake you boys up, but it's saddle time," Elise told the horses after lunch. She and Jolene each saddled her own horse, and Elise locked the truck and trailer.

"I'm ready, Mom." Jolene snapped closed the chin strap on her riding helmet. "How about you?"

Elise thumped the helmet on her own head. "Yes, I'm ready. I'm going to walk Tucker over to the mounting block to get on." She untied him and led him to the steps. Jolene untied Trick and put her left foot into the stirrup, then effortlessly swung into the saddle from the ground.

They walked the horses at a flat-footed walk for the first ten minutes to warm them up. When they reached the first turn to the right, the path widened and evened out. They moved the horses into their smooth walking horse gait, known as a running walk, that covered the ground rapidly. "Whoo hoo!" Jolene hollered. "This was worth getting up for. Thanks, Mom!"

They flew through the woods on their glide rides until they saw another rider ahead. They pulled up into a flat-footed walk. Even so, the walking horses covered more ground quicker than a trotting horse breed. They soon caught up to a young man on a brown and white paint horse. He turned to see a pretty teenage girl with long, blond hair and long legs sitting tall in the saddle and he did a double take.

Jolene was looking right back. She pretty much had her pick

of guys at her high school, so she was not easily impressed by one. This one, however, with his intense blue eyes and obvious love of horses, was catching her attention in a big way. "Hi," she said shyly.

"Hi," he answered just as shyly.

Jolene and Elise were riding single file. He pulled his horse to the side of the trail and fell in beside Jolene. "I'm Randy. Do you ride here much? Where else do you ride? Where do you go to school?" When he realized that he was babbling, he blushed red under his thick locks of black hair that needed a trim.

Elise watched from behind as Jolene answered his questions and asked him similar ones. They seemed to have forgotten that she was there. She picked up that his name was Randy, that he lived in the next county south, and that he was a freshman in college. *He's too old for her right now,* she thought. *This could be trouble.* She used her hand to slap a quarter-sized horse fly off of Tucker's neck. *Jolene's only sixteen and Randy must be nineteen.* Elise envisioned beer guzzling, weed-smoking, college fraternity parties, and insistence on sex in a back seat or dirty frat house bedroom.

"Come on, Jolene, let's boogie!" There was no room on the trail to pass the two kids riding abreast, so Elise moved Tucker into the weeds, ducked branches, moved in front, and urged Tucker into a fast running walk. Instead of leaving Randy behind as she had hoped, he moved his horse into a lope to keep up with Tucker and Tricked Out.

When they pulled up to a walk, Jolene and Randy picked up their conversation again. This time, Elise turned Tucker around to face them. "Hi, Randy, I'm Elise, Jolene's mother." She stretched out her hand, and Randy reached for it, but their horses were not close enough to connect.

Randy said, "Sorry. I'm Randy Reed. Pleased to meet you. You have a lovely daughter."

Elise thought, *I know you're aware of that and that's why I'm not giving you our last name. I hope Jolene didn't say it, either. I don't want you to see her again.* Out loud she said, "Thank you, Randy. What are you studying in school?"

"Biology and chemistry. I want to go to Ohio State veterinary school."

Well, that's a plus. He must be intelligent and motivated, but he's still too old for my daughter at this point in her life. "How interesting. Do you have family here?"

"Yes, Ma'am. I go to Kent State's Stark County branch because I live there with my folks. Do you ride here often? Where else do you ride?"

Uh, oh, here it comes, the where can I see her again questions. "Sometimes, Randy, just sometimes. We usually ride with a group of women, a whole bunch of us." *Maybe that will scare him away.* Elise wiped some sweat from her forehead just below her helmet.

"Mom, we usually only ride with them once a month on our campouts." Jolene turned to Randy. "The rest of the time we do day rides from home. We come here, we go to Walborn, Cuyahoga Valley, Brecksville, and Chagrin Metro Parks. Mom doesn't work, and I'm on summer break from school." Jolene hoped that sounded like she might be in college, too.

"You camp with the horses? So do I. Do you go to Beaver Creek?"

"Yes, we love it there! Do you?"

Randy's startling blue eyes twinkled. "What, love it, or camp there? Yes to both."

Jolene laughed.

"I'm only taking one course this summer on Mondays, Wednesdays and Fridays. Why don't we get together for some rides on Tuesdays or Thursdays, or both?"

Before she could answer Randy's question, Elise interrupted. "We have to move along and finish our ride. I have to stop at the grocery store and do some cooking when we get back home." She turned her horse around to head down the trail hoping Jolene would follow. She did, but Randy was right beside her. She heard them exchange phone numbers and Elise could only hope that they would both forget the other's number before they had a chance to write them down.

They rode the trail through the woods and circled back to the trucks. Randy hopped down from his horse and walked it over to Jolene. He held Tricked Out's bridle as Jolene swung off. They chatted quietly together until Elise called Jolene over to their trailer. "Come on, Honey, we have to go."

Randy tied his horse to his trailer and came over to help the women unsaddle their horses. He carried the saddles to the tack racks in the back of their trailer.

"Thank you, Randy," Elise said as she switched Tucker's bridle for his halter.

"No problem, Mrs. ...?" He looked expectantly at Elise with his astonishingly blue eyes.

"Parker, Elise Parker. Have a safe trip home, Randy."

"You, too, Mrs. Parker."

Randy turned to Jolene. He touched the back of her hand. "I'll give you a call." He turned to tend to his own horse.

Elise and Jolene loaded their horses and Jolene waved at Randy as they drove past him. *He does seem nice, but I hope that's the last we see of him,* Elise thought.

****

The first chance Elise had to talk privately, she telephoned Nancy. She closed her bedroom door and sat on the edge of her bed using her cell phone. She told Nancy about Jolene meeting Randy Reed and about how their age difference worried her since Jolene was so young.

"It would be horrible if he made Jolene pregnant and she couldn't finish school. He's just too old for her until she finishes her education." Elise lay back on the bed and clutched a pillow to her chest.

"Elise, you're borrowing trouble. So far they have only met once and now you have her pregnant. It doesn't work that way."

"Right, but like you said, so far. I'm worried that they're going to see each other."

"Does this Randy know how old Jolene is?"

"I don't know. I couldn't hear everything that was said. Maybe if he finds out how young she is, he won't be interested anymore." Suddenly Elise felt hopeful.

"Do you feel better now?" Nancy asked her. "I have to go see what my mother is up to. This is like watching a two-year-old who is constantly into something. It takes all my time."

"Yes, dear friend. Go. I do feel better. I'm probably worrying over nothing. You are going to the next campout, aren't you? Your sister is still coming to stay with your mother for that weekend?"

"Oh, yes, bless her heart. I'll be there. See you then."

They hung up and Elise went downstairs. Jolene was in the sun room off the kitchen talking on her cell phone. Elise decided to clean out the refrigerator so she could hear Jolene. She had cleaned one shelf when she figured out that Jolene was talking with a girlfriend. She felt better even though Jolene was telling her friend about meeting Randy and how she hoped he would call. At least Elise now knew that Randy had not yet called. Most guys never did call after telling a girl that they would.

Jolene hung up and walked into the kitchen.

"Hi, Mom. What are you doing?"

"Cleaning out the refrigerator." Elise set a jar of pickles on the counter next to the carton of milk and reached for the mustard and ketchup bottles. "Sit down here on the bar stool while I work." Elise wiped the shelf she had just emptied.

Jolene sat down and began handing her mother the food to put back on the clean refrigerator shelf.

"So, you haven't heard from Randy, huh?"

"Mom! What were you doing, listening to my conversation with Kendra? Can't I have some privacy around here?"

"Honey, I was cleaning out the refrigerator. You were right there in the sun room." Elise closed the refrigerator door and sat on a bar stool to face Jolene. "I do want to talk to you about Randy, anyway. Don't you think he's a little old for you?" Elise reached to tuck a long blond strand of Jolene's hair back behind her ear.

Jolene pushed her mother's hand away and frowned. "Mom, he's only three years older, and Dad is five years older than you. So what?"

"But that's different," Elise began.

"Different how? Because it's you and Dad and not me? That's not fair." The flat of Jolene's hand hit the counter.

"No, that's not it. Your father and I were both older when we began to date. We were both out of school. Right now you are only sixteen with only your driver's permit and no driver's license. Randy…"

Jolene interrupted. "That doesn't matter. If he takes me out, he can drive." Jolene gave her mother a challenging stare.

Elise picked up a pencil from the counter and twirled it in her fingers. "That's not it, Jolene. He has much more life experience than you. You have two more years of high school and then your college years. He could wreck your life."

"Oh, yeah, he is this horrible person, probably a murderer, who wants to be a veterinarian and loves his horse and the outdoors. How awful!"

Elise dropped the pencil. "I don't want you to date him. You just began dating yourself, and he's probably very experienced."

"Geez, Mom. Be reasonable!" Jolene jumped off the bar stool and slammed the door on the way out. Elise watched her daughter stomp to the barn.

I really messed up that talk. I'll have to have Marty handle it.

Marty did not handle it. Not the way Elise wanted him to, anyway. He supported Jolene.

Two days later, Randy did call her, and he asked her to a movie. Marty said that was fine, that she was raised right and would be able to handle herself. Elise asked what movie they were going to see and what time it would be over. She gave Jolene a curfew of half an hour after the end of the movie.

"But, Mom," Jolene complained. "What if he wants to take me to eat afterward? That's too early to come back home."

"Then have him pick you up earlier and go eat first, or eat popcorn at the theater."

"Mom! He'll think you're treating me like a kid! How embarrassing!"

"Well, you are just a kid. Only sixteen years ago you were in your cradle, and fourteen years ago you were just out of your diapers." Elise reminded her.

Jolene made a disgusting sound and marched to her room. Elise put her hands on her hips and glared at her husband who kept reading the newspaper and ignored her.

****

Jolene and Randy had two more dates after the first one. Elise was looking forward to the next campout to take Jolene away from Randy for the weekend. She toyed with extending this trip to a full week, but she wondered if it were true that absence does make the heart grow fonder.

Jolene wanted Randy to come on the campout with them, but

Elise said, "Absolutely not, and I don't care what your father says. It's a solid no, and that's that. This is our girls' weekend. No men!"

Jolene argued that Bristol had Bud there the last time, but Elise reminded her that Bud was already there on his own when Bristol met him.

On Monday afternoon, four days before their return to Beaver Creek, Lavern telephoned. "Listen, Elise, I'm sorry, but would you be willing to come to Harrison Forest instead of going to Beaver Creek? I had to get away from Charlie, and I'm in my truck with my horse trailer on my way to Harrison. I know it's a little farther, but farther from Charlie is better. I don't want him to find me, and he knows this is our weekend to camp. He'll probably go to Beaver Creek looking for me. I sure don't want to be there."

"Well, of course, Lavern. Are you afraid of him? Are you leaving him? Did you call the others?"

"Yes, yes, and yes, and everyone is willing to go to Harrison. Thank you, thank you. I'll explain everything that's happening when I see you. Just don't tell anyone where we're going. I don't want Charlie finding out, OK?" Lavern sounded stressed.

"Well, mostly OK. I'll have to tell Marty, but I'll make sure he knows not to tell anyone else. Don't worry. We will all be there Friday."

Lavern gave Elise her new cell phone number and they hung up.

It usually took Elise three or four days to make sure everything was ready for one of their trips. She always left the house clean and the laundry caught up. She always baked a ham or made a roast of beef to slice for sandwiches on the trip and to leave some for Marty's meals while they were gone.

Today she was baking cookies, planning her menus, making her grocery list, and changing the beds in the house and the trailer. Tomorrow she would go to the grocery, do the laundry, and pack her clothes. Jolene could pack her own. Wednesday she would clean the house and inside the trailer. Thursday Jolene could help her load their personal items, and the hay and grain for the horses. She would put fresh water in the trailer and bake a ham. After work, Marty would check the air pressure on the truck and trailer tires, and check the oil and coolant levels in the truck, and start the refrigerator. They would be ready to leave on Friday morning after loading last minute items like the groceries that needed to be refrigerated.

****

On Friday, Elise was up early to make breakfast for her family and to pack her husband's lunch. As soon as they said good-bye to Marty, Elise and Jolene showered, dressed, and loaded last-minute items onto the trailer. Jolene helped her mother hitch it to the truck.

Elise backed the trailer to the barn. Tucker was watching, his head over the gate to the pasture. Tricked Out was not in sight.

"Jolene, I wonder if Trick has figured out we're going riding and he's hiding. He could know because I backed the trailer to the barn." They walked to the fence and looked across the pasture. No second horse.

"Well, let's call them in to the barn to feed. He'll come in for his breakfast."

They went inside and dumped grain into their feed bins.

Tucker was waiting at the back barn door. Before Jolene could open it, Elise said, "I have an idea. I want to try something. I'm just curious as to what Tucker will do. Come on."

Jolene followed her mother back to the fence gate. Elise whistled. Tucker looked at them from behind the barn, confused. Elise whistled again. Tucker did not walk over, but he kept looking at her. "Tucker, where is Trick? Is Trick hiding? Show me where he is. Go on. Go get Trick."

"Mom, that's dumb. He doesn't know what you're saying, and he just wants in to eat his break..." Before Jolene could finish, Tucker moseyed over to the side of the pasture and behind the tool shed. He turned around and craned his neck to look back at them from behind the shed. "Well, how strange! I would never think he would leave before having his grain. Do you think Trick is back there and Tucker's showing us? I can't believe this!"

"I don't know. Let's go see."

They went through the gate and walked to the shed. There was Tricked Out standing behind it with Tucker. "Good boy, Tucker. You showed us where he is! You're amazing!" Elise stroked his neck. "Come on, guys. Time to eat."

They walked back to the barn and the horses followed. They rushed into their stalls for their breakfast as soon as the barn door opened.

"I guess I'm going to have to bring them in to eat before I move the trailer up," Elise said, laughing.

"Man, who would believe this?" Jolene was laughing, too.

After the horses finished their grain, they were loaded onto the trailer. Elise closed the trailer ramp while Jolene closed the barn door.

"Let's go to Harrison!" Elise said excitedly and punched the air as she went to climb into the truck cab.

"What?" Jolene looked horrified. "We're going to Beaver Creek, aren't we? Last time there everyone agreed to go back there for this weekend!"

Jolene stood there stricken. "Mom!"

Elise came around the truck to her daughter, and told her about Lavern's phone call and the need to keep their location secret.

"So you kept the change a secret from me, too? What, you think I would go running to tell Charlie? Come on, Mom, give me some credit! Does Dad know where we're going, or didn't you tell him, either?" Jolene stomped in a circle shouting at her mother.

"Jolene, I'm sorry. I guess I should have told you sooner. I've just been busy and didn't think about it until just now. Yes, your father knows where we will be."

"Geez, Mom, sometimes ..." Jolene did not finish that sentence. "OK, Harrison, then. I'll be right with you. I have to go to the bathroom." Jolene walked back to the house.

Elise climbed into the truck to wait. Ten minutes later they were on their way. They drove south then east through Canton and Carrolton, toward Scio, past Tappan Lake, to Cadiz, and north on Route 9 for four more miles to the Harrison State Forest horseman's camp. Elise was happy to arrive, not only to see that Lavern was safe, but also to end the drive with the quiet, pouty, Jolene.

CHAPTER 6
JUNE HORSE CAMPING

Elise and Jolene made their way down the long, paved entrance of the Harrison State Forest horseman's camp. At the end were two loops, one straight ahead, and one to the right. They turned onto the right loop, which took them around a central grassy area called The Commons that contained picnic tables and a restroom. Off to the right all around the loop were individual camping spots each with its own paved parking slab, a picnic table, and a picket line.

Elise had a big smile when she saw Lavern waving at them. She stopped the rig on the driveway, put the truck in idle, and jumped out. Jolene remained in the truck, still pouting.

Lavern and Elise hugged.

"I'm so glad to see you here safe and sound, Lavern. Where should I park? Will my rig fit on the spot next to yours?" Elise turned a three sixty looking around the camp.

"Yes, I was hoping you would come before Bristol gets here to be sure you could be next to me. It probably doesn't matter, though. We will mostly be hanging out together in The Commons when we aren't riding. We have an outdoor kitchen set up there under the Easy Up awning. Come on. Let's look at the camp site."

They walked up the hill to the spot next to Lavern's rig. The picket lines and picnic tables were downhill from the paved slab. "They're all like this on this side," Lavern told Elise. "On the other side of the loop, the picket lines are uphill from the parking slab. You can choose your site, and then register at the box hanging on the side of the restroom. Do you need any help?"

"No, Jolene can help me if I do. I'll take this spot next to you."

Elise backed her rig into the chosen spot with Jolene guiding her. They unloaded the horses and tied them to the picket line. Elise leveled the trailer with wood boards and the trailer jacks. Jolene stuffed a hay bag with a bale of hay and hung it from the picket line between the two horses, then she filled a water bucket from their water supply in the trailer and offered each horse a drink. She found the manure fork and cleaned out the horse stalls in the back of the trailer while Elise opened the vents and windows in the living quarters. Their camp was set up in less than an hour.

Elise made sandwiches, grabbed two apples and two of her home-baked cookies. "Come on, Jolene, wash your hands and let's go across to The Commons and have our lunch. I'll go see if Lavern wants to come over and eat with us."

Lavern joined them. They were just finishing when Bristol pulled in followed by Nancy. They both stopped their rigs in the road and climbed out to greet the others and to look over the camping spots. Only four of the sites were taken.

"So you're there, Lavern, and you're there, Elise. Who is there, and who's there?" Nancy pointed.

Lavern answered, "Those two are really neat ladies who work for a school system and have the summer off like I do. They live here all summer, work on the trails, and ride! I'll introduce you when they get back from their ride. Their names are Cadey, and Brianna, who likes to be called Bree. I've been here since Monday evening. We've had a campfire every night, and I've worked on trail with them every day, so I had a chance to get to know them. You'll like them."

Bristol and Nancy each picked out their spots, parked, and set up their camps. It was two o'clock by the time they were finished and ready to ride. Everyone saddled up, mounted, and met in the grassy middle of camp.

Lavern pointed out the two bridle trails leaving camp. "Come on, let's go up this way." She turned Lacy up the camp road. At the top of the hill, she turned into the woods on the Gibby trail. "This trail is named in honor of Wilbur T. Gibson who laid out the bridle trails here at Harrison and also at Bark Camp," Lavern turned around in her saddle and told them.

"Yeah, yeah, always the school teacher," Bristol muttered.

The trail was narrow, and the women had to watch so that they did not hit their knees on the trees. They wound single file up the rocky hill. The horses strained until finally reaching the top. They turned onto the blue trail which was wider and smoother. The riders followed the blue trail until it came to a lake at the bottom of a hill where they were able to water the horses. The lake reflected the blue sky, and several dead trees rose from the water like sculptures. As the horses lined up to drink, two riders came down the hill toward the lake from the yellow trail.

Lavern waved. "Hey, here come Bree and Cadey!"

The horses finished drinking, and the women watched as Bree and Cadey approached. They looked to be in their fifties, tan, brown hair, happy smiles. Bree wore a baseball cap, and Cadey wore an Australian outback hat. They were in blue jeans and short-sleeved shirts. Lavern made introductions.

"Welcome to our favorite place to ride," Cadey told the group. "Have we met before?" she asked Bristol.

"I doubt it," Bristol said without trying to explore whether they had met in the past.

"Yes, something about you is familiar, but anyway, you're all welcome to come to our campfire in the middle circle that we call The Commons tonight if it doesn't rain," Bree invited them. "I have makings for S'mores."

Everyone agreed that would be fun.

Bree and Cadey watered their horses as the others rode away to continue their ride down the blue trail. "There's something about Bristol what's her name." Cadey was trying to remember.

"Yeah. Bristol Monarch. That name is familiar."

"Uh, huh. That's it. Isn't she the one who…"

"Yes, she is. She's the one who was in that other horse club and they…"

"Yeah, they kicked her out."

"Uh, huh. The board voted her out when she was president of the club."

"Right! She was president and the club started losing so many members they got rid of her."

Bree and Cadey shook their heads and turned their horses toward camp.

Lavern had already led the other four riders up the hill and back into the woods on the narrow yellow trail. The scenery was beautiful. The woods were thick with deciduous trees and evergreens. The ground was covered with old leaves, ferns, stones, and broken branches. Birds were chirping. The sky was turquoise blue and cloudless. The hoof beats of the horses were pleasing to their ears. It was a great day to ride.

Lavern turned in her saddle and told the others that the wider blue trail was the main trail in the system with the other trails looping off of and back to the blue trail on each side of it.

"Yes, that's right. They do," Bristol said.

When the yellow trail crossed the blue trail, the riders turned left onto the blue, still headed away from camp, and moved their horses into their faster, smooth gaits. They slowed only when the trail went downhill.

At the end of the blue trail before turning onto the green trail, the group decided to ride back to camp. By the time they finished the ride and took care of the horses, it would be time to make dinner.

****

Everyone in camp gathered in The Commons for a potluck dinner. Nancy, always willing to say a blessing before the meal, first asked the group if anyone else would like to do it.

After two seconds of silence, Bristol spouted, "Well, *I* have no trouble talking to the Lord. *I'll* say the blessing." After her short prayer, they lined up to fill their plates buffet-style.

When the dinner was finished and everything cleaned up, each of them tended to her horse, feeding, watering, and mucking the picket lines before dark. It did not rain, and the ladies gathered in the grassy middle again to have their campfire and eat S'mores.

Lavern caught her friends up to date on her life. "So I filed for divorce, found an apartment, and moved out. I'm going to stay here for the rest of the summer to keep away from Charlie. That should give him time to calm down before school starts and I have to be back to teach."

Bristol picked at a burned marshmallow on her stick and said to Lavern, "So you finally took my advice and left that jerk."

"What makes you think I left him because of what *you* said? " Lavern responded with heat.

Nancy quickly jumped in. "You know, Lavern, it's kind of funny. You actually moved out and *then* found your apartment." She told the others, "Lavern had all her belongings boxed up and in her horse trailer."

"Yes, and now they're still boxed up sitting in my new apartment."

"Ric bought me a Martin guitar," Bristol announced, changing the subject. "Bud and I have been playing music and singing together. They really like us at the open mic at the Amped Up. We get a lot of applause, and people ask us to come back all the time."

No one responded to this. Bree picked up the long forks used for toasting the marshmallows and closed the box of graham crackers. Cadey threw another log on the fire and stirred it. Sparks shot skyward.

"So, how is your mother doing, Nancy?" Elise asked.

Nancy was thoughtful. "Mom is getting along better than I am. She seems to be unaware of having this disease. She sure is a handful, and my sister is going to have a rude awakening about it this weekend while she takes care of her."

Elise licked gooey marshmallow from her fingers and complemented Cadey and Bree on the condition of the trails they had ridden that afternoon. "You do a lot of work here keeping them up."

"Yeah, well, it's our hobby, and it gives us a chance to live out here and ride our horses," Cadey told them. "The ranger likes the camp to be occupied between weekends to keep druggies and lovers away. Anyway, we have help from time to time from our Ohio Horsemen Council group."

"Do you know what that is?" Bree asked them.

"Of course, we know. We have an OHC chapter in our county," Bristol snapped.

"The ranger told us the governor wants to log some of the trails here at Harrison, but we don't think he will ever have that done. There were thousands of volunteer hours to make these trails and to maintain them. I think we're safe," Bree said.

"That's right," Bristol chimed in.

There was silence for a few minutes. Now and then they could hear a horse moving about on a picket line, a horse snorting, and the fire cracking.

Nancy broke the silence. "Elise, did you have the muffler fixed on your truck? You got here before I did, so I didn't hear your truck when you came in."

Elise nodded her head and was about to speak when Jolene piped up, "Yes, she did, and before she took it in to be fixed, she vacuumed out the whole cab, front and back, and then sprayed most of a bottle of Febreze."

The women chuckled and Nancy asked, "What, you were making it nice for, the mechanic?"

Lavern asked, "Why did you do that?"

"Go ahead. Tell them, Mom."

Elise confessed, "Well, the weekend before, I went to the animal auction at Roger's Flea Market and bought a bunch of live chickens. I had to put their crates in the truck cab with me. There were feathers everywhere, and some other stuff that fell through the crates, and it smelled really bad in there."

Now the ladies were laughing.

"So," Bree asked, "did you want the chickens for their eggs? How many did you buy?"

"Oh, no, I bought them to resell them. I sold them for twice what I paid for them."

"That's right," Bristol said. "You can do that with the animal auction."

Cadey moved her chair away from the fire smoke. "Hey, how do you gals keep your horses? I mean, are they stalled all the time or are they always in the pasture, or what?"

Lavern swallowed the last of her S'more. "I board Lacy, and Slade keeps the horses outside all summer. In the winter he leaves them out during the day and brings them in at night."

Jolene looked at her mother who said nothing, so Jolene answered for them. Her mood had improved during the trail ride. "We keep our horses outside all the time unless it gets too cold or when it rains while it's too cold. They pretty much only come into the barn to eat."

Nancy weighed in. "All summer Bright Beauty stays outside at night and in the barn during the heat of the day. All winter, it's the opposite. She stays outside all day and in during the cold of the night."

Bristol threw another log on the fire and sparks exploded. She sat back down. "I put Hot Stuff outside every day and bring her inside every night all year. It doesn't matter what the weather is."

A discussion ensued about the pros and cons of their various methods. Finally Bristol said, "Let's save time and just say that I'm right. My horse is very healthy."

Bree and Cadey each looked at Bristol then looked at each other. Bree shrugged. "I think I'll turn in now. See you tomorrow. Anyone who wants to work on trail with us is more than welcome. We start at eight."

"Yeah, I'm going to turn in now, too," Cadey agreed. Good night everyone." Bree and Cadey folded their chairs and walked back to their trailers to tend their horses and go to bed.

"So these are the two gals you *like*?" Bristol asked Lavern.

"Yes, they are!" Lavern answered firmly, *and I would choose to spend my time with them before being with you,* she thought. "I'm going to bed, too. Good night." She folded her chair and left the fire before she would say something to Bristol that she might regret.

Elise, Jolene, and Nancy also said their good nights, and left Bristol to watch the fire by herself.

****

Saturday morning everyone was up early to tend to the horses and to gather at a picnic table in The Commons for their breakfast. Elise fried bacon, Nancy hard-boiled a dozen eggs and brought orange juice, Lavern pan-fried toast to serve with her apple butter, and Bristol contributed store-bought sweet rolls. Cadey had a pot of coffee for the group, and Bree said she would make blueberry pancakes for everyone the next morning to go with the sausage Cadey planned to fry.

Elise was pleased that Jolene had climbed out of bed without a fuss and that she was in a good mood this morning. She had fed and watered the horses and mucked the manure from under their feet without being asked, while Elise fried the bacon. There were two seats left at the picnic table when Jolene went to sit down. Both seats faced away from the road coming into the campground. Jolene asked Nancy to trade sides with her.

Surprised, Nancy said, "Sure, Honey, I can sit over there."

Jolene thanked her and sat down.

With breakfast nearly over, Jolene's good mood also seemed to be ending. When Bree suggested that it was time to saddle up if anyone was going to help trim trees back from the green trail, Jolene frowned.

"Don't you want to go with them?" her mother asked her. "We don't have to get off the horses. We're just going to use our hand nippers to cut back the small branches growing over the trail."

"Pack a lunch because the green trail is at the end of the system, and one section of it goes to the regular RV and tenting camp ground. We can ride there and eat at a picnic table," Cadey told them between sips of coffee.

"How long will it take until we're back, then?" Jolene nearly whined.

Suddenly she brightened and jumped up. "Oh, look! Here comes Randy! He must have driven down for a day ride or maybe to camp!"

All heads turned to see a beat-up black Ford truck, pulling a rusty, red, two-horse, bumper-pull, coming down the camp road.

"Jolene!" her mother barked. "Did you know he was coming? Did you invite him here?" Elise was angry with her daughter.

"No, Mom, I did not invite him," Jolene said sheepishly. She started to run to the road to greet Randy, but Elise grabbed her arm.

"Jolene, what's going on?"

"Oh, Mom, maybe I did tell him we would be here instead of Beaver Creek, but he decided to come on his own." Jolene broke her mother's grasp and ran happily to Randy.

Elise put her head in her hands. Lavern touched Elise's shoulder and told her, "You can't stop love with good advice. Sometimes it just has to play out."

"That's right," Bristol said.

Nancy encouraged Elise with a pat on her hand and a reminder, "You brought her up well, and you keep her in your prayers. Don't worry. Give this situation over to God. Remember the 46th Psalm that tells us God is our refuge and strength, a helper who is always found in times of trouble. We are not supposed to be afraid 'though the earth trembles and the mountains topple into the depth of the seas.'"

"That's just it," Elise replied as she watched Randy and Jolene embracing. "I'm afraid he is going to tumble her mountain and find the depth of her seas."

The women at the table chuckled, but Nancy hushed them and said a quick prayer out loud. "Lord, please be with these two young people and help them to make good and pure decisions. Help Elise to find peace in this situation and to give wise counsel to her daughter. Amen."

"Amen," Lavern echoed her.

Bristol left the table to pack her lunch and to saddle her horse. The other women cleaned up after the breakfast before packing their own lunches and saddling their horses.

Before they were finished, Bud Fisher surprised everyone but Bristol by roaring into camp, spitting gravel, his silver bumper-pull stock trailer nearly fishtailing behind his blue Chevy truck. He slowed when he saw Bristol's camp and went to speak with her. The women watched from the common area as Bud unloaded his tall, black horse and walked it to the picket line next to Bristol's camp. Bristol helped him back his rig onto the pad next to hers.

Cadey nodded toward Bristol and Bud. "Well, I guess we have another rider today. Maybe he'll help us with the trail work."

"Now we have two men on our ladies' weekend," Elise complained.

Bree said, "Whatever, but he should slow down pulling that rig."

Lavern wiped the picnic table with a dish cloth and told the others, "I used to have a rig like that, a bumper-pull stock trailer and a cap on the back of my truck so I could sleep without getting wet." A stock trailer had from two to four open spaces, or slits, running the length of the sides of the trailer. They were each about five inches wide. There were no living quarters or stalls, just an open space inside.

Lavern continued, "I had a sun shower that held five gallons of water that would heat when I laid it in the sun. Then I tied it high in my trailer to use it. I figured that the open slits were high enough that no one would see in. One day I was all soaped up when I heard a man go, 'Oh!' I looked up and saw this cowboy on his tall horse and he *could* see in! I was so embarrassed that when I dressed, I couldn't come out for a long time. After that trip, I started shopping for my gooseneck with living quarters."

When everyone was saddled and mounted, they met in The Commons. Jolene introduced Randy to the group, and Bristol introduced Bree and Cadey to Bud.

"I'm sorry I was kind of late this morning. I hope I didn't hold you up any," Bud apologized. "I took the scenic route," he explained.

Bree, still miffed, told him, "I don't think any route would have been scenic the way you were driving!"

The others laughed good naturedly.

"Anyway, if you're riding with us, it's lucky you came in time because we didn't know you were coming. We would have been gone," Nancy told Bud.

"Well, I would have waited for you," Bristol cooed and all but batted her eyelashes. "We aren't riding with you, anyway, Nancy. We're going on our own. Come on, Bud." Bristol turned her horse and went up the road and into the woods. Bud followed her after an apologetic look at the others.

"Mom, Randy and I are going to ride alone, too."

"Oh, no, you aren't, Jolene. I think we should all help Bree and Cadey do the trim work on the trail. I bet they can use Randy's muscle power to do some heavier work, too."

"We can use him, all right," Bree said as she turned her horse up the road to the trail head, Cadey right behind her.

Lavern was next on Lacy, then Nancy on Bright Beauty. Jolene was hanging back until Elise said, "You two go on." She wanted to keep an eye on her daughter and Randy. Jolene moved Tricked Out into his running walk to catch up to the others, Randy trotting right behind her on his brown and white paint. Elise sighed and moved out on Tucker.

The riders enjoyed the ride through the woods for a couple of hours when they came to the area where they would do the trail work. From the backs of their horses the women used hand nippers to trim off small branches growing over the trail above them. Randy dismounted, and used a small hand saw to cut new-growth trees that were from one to three inches in diameter and crowding the trail, before they could grow into knee knockers.

The volunteers had the Harrison Forest trails in such good shape that they completed their work in less than two hours. They took a lunch break then enjoyed the ride back to camp. They did not run into Bristol and Bud.

At camp they each took care of their horses, unsaddling, washing sweat from them, watering them, hanging new hay bales, mucking out from under the picket line, and cleaning mud from their tack. It was now late afternoon and camp was quiet with people reading or resting at their campsite, or talking at the picnic table in the middle.

Cadey was laying a fire ready for the evening when a saddled but riderless black horse galloped into camp. Nancy shouted, "That's Rocky, Bud's horse! Something's wrong! We need to go find him!" Cadey shouted to Bree to saddle up again. Elise shouted to Jolene, who was napping in the gooseneck, that they needed to saddle up again to look for a downed rider. Lavern threw down her book and leaped from her lawn chair to saddle her horse.

Before the women finished tacking their horses, Bristol rode into camp. The women gathered around her, all shouting excitedly at once.

"What happened?"

"Where's Bud?"

"His horse came back to camp."

"Are you all right?"

"Is Bud OK?"

"Is Bud hurt?"

"Yeah, Yeah, I'm OK and so is Bud. Rocky ran off when Bud got down to, to ah, to pee. He's walking back now. I thought I would see if Rocky came back to camp and pony him back to Bud so he doesn't have to walk all the way."

The women were relieved to know that no one had been injured. They unsaddled again as Bristol rode Hot Stuff over to Rocky, attached a lead line to his trail bridle, and rode off with Rocky following.

****

Camp quieted down again. Bree was combing her horse's tail when Cadey joined her. "Look at this huge knot, Cadey. I've been working at untangling this knot for two weeks, and I can't get it worked out, not even with Cowboy Magic that should untangle anything."

"Let me see." Cadey took the comb from Bree. The knot was a huge tangled mass high on the underside of the tail, with long, straight hair hanging from the knot. It was gooey with the conditioner.

After ten minutes, Cadey told Bree, "You're just going to have to bite the bullet and cut this knot out. It's such a mess that it will never untangle. Go get scissors and let's do this."

Bree frowned, but she knew it was true. It took them several minutes to cut the tangle free. Finally Cadey held up the tangled clump with three feet of straight hair streaming from it. "Look at this. Wow!"

"Give it to me. I'll throw it out." Bree reached for it, but Cadey held it away.

"Oh, no, it's too good to just throw it away. We have to do something with it."

"Like what?"

"I don't know. Think of something, Bree." Cadey held the knot and stroked the length of hair.

"OK, I know!" Bree was starting to become excited. "This is black, and Bristol's black and white horse has a mostly black tail. We have to do something to her with this."

Cadey put the horse hair on the fender of Bree's trailer. They sat down on her lawn chairs.

"I've got it!" said Cadey, excited. "Let's put the thing under her horse while it's on the picket line and make her think her horse is losing its hair. It should freak her out since she's so much into appearance."

"Oh, yeah, that would be good, but we have to set it up. At supper we have to talk about how horses lose their hair when they're stressed. Then when she sees it, she'll already have that mind set."

"OK. Should we bring the others in on it?" Cadey pushed a lock of hair off of her forehead.

"No, I'm not sure they would go along, especially not Nancy. But maybe Jolene would. Yeah, let's clue Jolene in."

They found Jolene sitting with Randy at his campsite. They shared their plan with them, and both agreed to help. They decided that Randy would be the one to plant the horse tangle under Hot Stuff's feet just before supper as soon as he saw Bristol walking to The Commons. During the meal, they would try to bring up the topic of stress related hair loss as naturally as they could.

At six o'clock everyone was sitting at one of the picnic tables in the center of camp with the food on another table for their buffet-style pot-luck. Randy winked at Jolene when he sat down beside her to let her know that he had successfully placed the horse hair under Hot Stuff. Jolene nodded at Cadey and Bree when she had their attention. The game was on.

Nancy asked if anyone would like to give a blessing before they ate. Bristol immediately snapped, "I will! I talk to the Lord all the time. I'm not afraid to talk to him here."

After the prayer, they loaded their plates and sat back down. Elise told everyone how it seemed that her horse Tucker showed them where Tricked Out was hiding behind the shed. The rest laughed as Bristol said, "Oh, come on. That's stupid. You know he wasn't thinking that. It's called anthropomorphic when you give human traits to animals."

Elise burned and turned away from Bristol. She asked Lavern about how she was coping with her thoughts about her divorce.

Lavern replied that she was stressed, not over the divorce, but over fear that Charlie might find her and possibly hurt her.

This was the opening Cadey and Bree had been waiting for. Cadey said, "You know, Lavern, stress is not good for you. It can do all kinds of things to your body. You will have to take extra good care of yourself through all of this."

"You are so right," Bree added. "My mother's friend was going through a stressful time. and her hair began to fall out. She had really beautiful hair, too. It was long and curly, and so much fell out that it left a bald spot right on top. It was awful for her."

Unwittingly Nancy added to the set up. "I know stress contributes to hair loss. Since Mom has been living with us, I have lost a lot more hair. I was going to discuss it with my doctor my next visit."

"It happens to stressed horses, too," Randy said.

"Randy should know. He's studying to be a veterinarian," Jolene told the group.

"I also saw it first hand in a young horse some people had on trail for the first time ever. They went on an all-day ride. It was just too much for that young horse its first time out. It lost a long hank of hair in just a couple hours after they came back from the trail." Randy stood up to take a second helping of Lavern's homemade cheesy potatoes.

The conversation continued better than the instigators had hoped with everyone contributing stories they knew about people or animals with hair loss from stress. When Randy summed it up, "Yeah, there can be significant hair loss from stress," and Bristol said, "Yes, you're right," Cadey nearly choked on her pie, and Jolene and Bree giggled.

Bristol stood up and said to Bud, "Come on. Let's go get our guitars while the ladies clean up. We need to tend our horses, and then we can tune up and be ready to sing at the camp fire."

All of the women were miffed, but it was Elise who confronted Bristol. "We all have horses to tend to. Why don't you help us clean up here?"

"What are you complaining about?" Bristol asked her. "You have Jolene to help you." With that, Bristol walked away. Bud looked sheepish, but he followed her. Lavern, Elise, and Nancy began to put away the supper things and clean up the tables. Cadey, Bree, Jolene, and Randy stood watching Bud and Bristol walk up the hill.

Bud had just left Bristol's side to continue up the road to his campsite when Bristol screamed and pointed toward her horse. Bud hurried to her side. Jolene, Cadey and Bree were laughing hard. Randy was smiling. The other women stared up the hill wondering what was going on and whether they were needed to help.

Elise grabbed Jolene's arm. "Why are you laughing? Do you know what's happening? What's going on?"

"Mom, Bristol the know-it-all is just getting like, some

payback. Don't worry. No one is hurt and nothing's wrong."

By then, Bud had his arm around Bristol and they had walked up to the horse. Bud leaned over and picked up the tangled black horse hair. Bristol was combing through Hot Stuff's tail with her fingers.

"Jolene, did you cut Hot Stuff's tail? What did you do, young lady?" Elise was mortified that her daughter would do such a thing.

"Don't worry," Bree told her. "This was not Jolene's idea, and she didn't do anything."

"That's right. It's hair from Bree's horse's tail and we just put it under Bristol's horse." Cadey told them the whole story as they watched Bud try to calm an agitated Bristol. Finally Elise laughed, then Lavern laughed, then Nancy. They were all laughing when Bristol looked down the hill and saw them.

"Uh, oh. We've been caught," Lavern told the group.

"We sure have," Elise said, "but maybe she'll be mad enough at us that she won't come to the campfire tonight and we won't have to listen to her sing."

"Don't count on it. I think she's proud enough of her singing that she won't let anything stop her from showing off," Nancy told them.

It turned out that Nancy was correct. Just before dark, Bristol and Bud came walking down the hill, Bud carrying both guitars. The others were already sitting around the campfire in their lawn chairs, their horse chores completed for the night. They would only have to check on them before bed, and offer them more water.

"Is that her husband?" Bree asked watching Bristol and Bud.

"No, she's married to a very nice man. We met him a few times. It's a wonder he stays with her the way she treats him," Elise answered her. "Our monthly campouts are supposed to be for girls only. I don't know what's gotten into her, but I don't like the looks of it."

The thread of that conversation ended because Bristol and Bud came into hearing distance. They sat down and opened their guitar cases without asking if anyone wanted to hear them play. They had worked out a few songs together, and they did sound better than the first time they played at Beaver Creek, but Bristol did not yet know how to play the guitar well. She had to follow Bud for the chord changes, and she was always a little behind in the timing. Sometimes she just stopped playing to sing. They were playing right at the fire circle, and they were loud enough that it was difficult for the others to have a conversation.

Elise put her head back and closed her eyes. She wondered about continuing to bring Jolene around Bristol, who definitely was not a good role model. When the music ended, she opened her eyes. Neither Jolene nor Randy were in the fire circle any longer. Elise sat up straight.

"Has anyone seen Jolene? When did she leave?"

"She and Randy walked toward his camp about ten minutes ago," Bristol told her with a smirk.

Elise jumped up from her chair and began to fold it. Lavern touched Elise's arm and said, "Wait, let me handle it. I have some things to say to her."

Elise nodded, unfolded her chair, and sat back down. Still upset, but trusting her friend, she watched Lavern walk off toward Randy's campsite.

From the road, Lavern saw them sitting in front of Randy's trailer. They were holding hands and talking quietly. Lavern smiled and kept walking. She walked the loop back to the campfire and told Elise not to worry about them. "They're just sitting there talking. I'll talk to Jolene in a little while. Give them a little time to get to know each other. Maybe one will decide the other is not for them before it goes much farther."

As some of the women began to fold their chairs and leave the fire, Jolene came back and told her mother that she was ready for bed. Lavern told Jolene that she would walk her back to her camp. Elise stayed by the fire giving Lavern the opportunity to talk to Jolene.

"Honey," Lavern began, "do you know about my situation with Charlie?"

"Well, a little bit. I know you left him, and now he's like, so angry that you're afraid he'll hurt you."

"Do you understand why I left him?"

"Not really. Oh, careful," Jolene warned as Lavern nearly tripped on the uneven ground in the dark. "I don't understand how you can love someone so much that you marry him, and then you like don't want him anymore."

"It does seem to be a mystery sometimes how love can fade away, and sometimes that's all it is, just two people growing apart. But sometimes, when a person does not choose their mate carefully, they can find themselves in a trap that ruins their life until they find the courage and independence to break free. Sometimes a spouse can be unfaithful, or constantly cruel, and you have to decide whether it's worth staying with them."

"Yeah, I guess I can see that. I met Ric a couple of times and he seems really nice. Can you imagine being married to Bristol and having to live with her all the time? Yuck! But didn't he know how mean she is when he dated her, let alone married her?"

They reached Jolene's campsite and Jolene invited Lavern inside. They settled themselves at the small table and continued to talk.

"Usually a mean person can control themselves enough to put on a good front when it is very important to them. They can make you believe in them, believe that they are this good person they are pretending to be. Then, when they have you trapped, the real person comes out and it's too late for you."

"Is that what happened with Charlie?"

"Yes. He was so sweet and kind and loving until he had me. Then he began controlling me. I went along with most things just to avoid fighting with him. The thing is, it's growing worse. The counselor told me it probably would, and that I would have to be careful because his need to control would probably go from emotional abuse to physical abuse."

"Here's the thing," Lavern continued. "If I didn't have my education, my teaching degree, I would still be trapped in an abusive relationship. I just want you to be aware that sometimes men are not what they seem, and probably women either. I hope and pray that you will put a priority on independence. Finish your education and be able to make your own independent living. Be careful and take your time about choosing a mate. But if he turns out to be abusive, or unfaithful, or something that you just can't live with, you don't have to. Plan for the best, but prepare for the worst. Do you understand?"

"Sort of." Jolene was tired and she rubbed her eyes. They could hear Elise taking a hay bale out of the trailer to hang for the horses. "Are you telling me that you think Randy would be one of those, an abuser, or something?"

"Oh, no, Honey. Not at all. For all I know he would make you or someone else a wonderful husband. But that's the thing. I don't know, and you don't know. It's way too early to tell. I'm definitely not telling you to leave a husband for petty reasons. I'm just giving you loving advice to be careful. Don't get pregnant until you're ready to start your family. Finish school and be prepared for an independent career. Take lots of time dating anyone you're interested in. Give them lots of time for their true colors to show, and I'm talking three or four years. If it's real, it will wait, and you can have fun dating. Now give me a hug and go help your mother with the horses."

****

Sunday morning at the group breakfast, Jolene looked unhappy even though she was sitting next to Randy. Lavern, concerned, asked her what was wrong.

"We have to leave early," Jolene told her as she pushed her breakfast around her plate.

"Why?"

"Because last night on the picket line Tricked Out caught his hind foot in the lead rope, and we think he pulled a muscle. He's limping on it this morning. I can't ride him, and Mom won't go off and leave me in camp alone, so we're going home."

Randy offered, "She's lucky that they realized what was happening right away, or the horse could have been dead by this morning."

"Yes, I think so, too," agreed Elise. "We were both asleep. A strange noise woke me up. I kept listening, trying to identify it. Finally I decided to check on the horses. I went out with my flashlight and saw Trick on the ground on his back with his neck stretched way high against the lead rope, and his hind leg stretched up in the air. The lead rope was wrapped around his leg. The noise was him pulling against the picket line trying to free himself. The whites of his eyes were showing. He was in a bad predicament, and he knew it."

"I know, right? Mom tried to unhook the lead rope from his halter, but it was stretched so tight that it wouldn't unlatch. She came in to get a knife, and that's when she woke me up. I went out with her and held the light while she cut the rope. It took her awhile to saw through it! I was scared."

"So, when he was free, he just lay there for awhile," Elise continued. "We were afraid he might have broken a bone. We had to encourage him to get up. Finally he did. We walked him a little bit, and although he favored that hind foot, he seemed to be OK. I think he may have pulled a muscle. I'm surprised none of you heard us in the night."

"That's too bad, Jolene," Nancy told her. "I'm sure he'll be OK, though. I'm just glad your mother found him in time."

"I know, right?" Jolene shuddered at the thought.

"Yes, that would have been awful to find him in the morning," Lavern said, adding *dead* in her mind. "You know, I kind of woke up a little around two this morning. I heard some of the horses whinnying. It must have been when you were walking Trick."

"That was really stupid of you to tie the lead rope too loose so that he could tangle his foot in it," Bristol chided. "I mean, how stupid can you be?"

Nancy saw the stricken look on Jolene's face and said, "Can it, Bristol. You've been nothing but snappish and sarcastic all weekend."

"Be glad you at least got that!" Bristol snapped back. Even Bud looked at her with amazement as she threw down her napkin and left the table.

Nancy stopped Bristol in her tracks as she said in a voice that sounded more patient than she felt, "That's what I mean, Bristol. I've been patient with you, but I'm done with it. You need to get down on your knees and ask God to help you change your mean and sarcastic ways. God loves you even when you're completely unlikeable, but it's really difficult for us. I know you say you talk to the Lord, but you really need to open your heart to God. The more you do, the more your anger and hurt will melt away. I know you have insecurities, but they are no excuse not to be a kind and gentle person. If you disgust yourself, instead of taking it out on other people, ask God to show you His love. Then maybe you can learn to love both yourself and others. I think you should start by apologizing to Jolene."

Bristol crossed her arms in front of her heaving chest. "I don't know who you think you are, Nancy, to lecture me that way, but you want an apology? OK. How's this? I've got to stop saying 'How stupid can you be.' Too many people are taking it as a challenge."

Bristol looked at the shocked faces in front of her and continued, "Oh, that wasn't a real apology, was it? OK, how's this. I'm sorry I hurt your feelings when I called you stupid, Jolene. I really thought you already knew. Now, does anyone else have an opinion about my life? If so, raise your hand, and then put it over your mouth."

Bristol stalked off before anyone in the shocked group could say anything. Bud was embarrassed and left for the men's room.

"Are you OK?" Randy asked Jolene.

"Yeah, I'm OK. I think I have like an adrenaline rush, though. That was intense. I know that if someone I respected said those things to me that I would be very upset, but since it's Bristol, I guess it doesn't matter that much, especially since everyone pretty much knows what she's like. Yeah, it's definitely her, not me."

Randy put his arm around her shoulders and hugged her.

Elise said, "Honey, I'm proud of you. And, of course, you're not stupid."

The others agreed.

By unspoken consensus, the group continued to sit at the picnic table to watch what would happen next with Bristol who was at her campsite slamming things around. As they watched, Bud joined her, and they talked for a few minutes. Then Bud went to his own camp and started packing up.

"Do you think he's had enough of her?" Lavern asked the group. "He shouldn't be sniffing around a married woman this way, anyway."

"I don't know. It looks like she's mucking under the picket line. Is she going to leave now, too, or is she just cleaning up before the ride?" Bree asked. "I hope she doesn't want to ride with us again. *I've* certainly had enough of her. How long did you say you all have been friends?"

"I'm afraid a bit too long," Nancy answered. "I've been praying for her to have compassion for others and to have a healing from her anger and insecurities. I'm also praying for myself to be able to understand her and to forgive her surliness. She's a difficult person, but she does have some goodness in her that comes out now and then."

Lavern interrupted Nancy. "I think what you thought was her rare good side was really a hypocritical veneer of civility."

Nancy ignored Lavern's remark and continued. "I thought I could help by being her friend and praying for her, but she does not have an open and receptive heart at this time."

"Are you saying that God hasn't answered your prayers for her?" Jolene asked.

"No, not at all. I'm saying that God is still working on her, but her heart is closed off right now. In the meantime, God *has* answered my prayers for a peaceful relationship with her, although in a different way than I expected, by removing her from my life and giving me peace that way. See, she's loading Hot Stuff into her trailer. She isn't going to ride with us. I know you girls have not really wanted to have her around for a long time. As far as I'm concerned, Bristol has made her choice today to leave our group. We don't need to inform her about our next trips. I think we have all tried to be patient and understanding, but I do hope that you will keep her in your prayers and ask God to help her find her way to peace. She's a very unhappy person."

"Better pray for peace for poor Ric, too," Jolene said, and everyone agreed.

As they sat at the picnic table watching, Bristol started driving her rig down the camp road followed by Bud in his rig.

Elise jumped up and ran into the road, blocking Bristol's way. Bristol slowed to a stop and lowered her truck window. "What?" she asked rudely.

142

"I just want you to know," Elise told her, "that you're not welcome in our group anymore. None of us like how nasty you are with us, and I cannot tolerate you treating my daughter that way. You're not a good role model for her either, going on with Bud like this."

"Oh, for Pete's sake!" Bristol said, rolling up her window and cutting Elise off from saying anything more. She stepped on the gas causing Elise to jump back to avoid being run over.

Good she thought while walking back to her friends, *I'm glad I told her. She thought she was leaving our group on her own terms, but now she knows it's us who don't want her.*

As Elise rejoined them, Nancy's cell phone rang. The group could only hear one side of the conversation.

"Hello?"

"Oh, hi, is everything all right? Is Mom OK?"

"Well, yes, it *is* that hard. I've been trying to tell you. Now you know, and believe me, I appreciate your being there so I can do these monthly campouts. I just wish you lived closer so you could help more often, but I understand. We all do what we can."

"What? Really? You would? You will? You're not kidding me?"

"Oh, my gosh! Oh, Sis! You're the greatest! You're really going to? Oh, wow! Oh, my gosh! That is really great news! I love you, Sis."

"Yeah. OK. See you this evening. We'll make plans. Huh? What? I can? You will? Geez, Sis. OK. Two more days then, if it's OK with Harry."

"It is? You're sure? OK then. You really *are* the greatest! Love you. Bye."

Nancy clicked off her phone. A grin slowly spread across her whole face as the others watched her expectantly.

"What?" Elise asked.

"My sister is going to move up here to help me take care of Mom! That's the best news. I'm so excited and so relieved! She's a nurse and she said she can find a job up here really fast. Her apartment lease is up in two months and she can move then. She said that after looking after Mom for just three days, she doesn't know how I do it. Oh, my gosh! She's coming to help! Oh, my gosh!" Nancy, giddy with joy, did a happy dance on the grass.

"Then, to top it off, she said she phoned work and made arrangements to take a week's vacation and stay longer on this trip. She said I could spend the week camping down here if I wanted to, but I told her I would stay just two extra days. I don't have enough food for me, or hay for the horse, for a whole week. Anyway, two extra days will be nice, and then I can spend some time with my sis the rest of the week." The others smiled, happy for her.

Elise, Jolene, and Randy left to break camp and go home. Nancy, Lavern, Bree, and Cadey left to saddle for the ride. Bristol and Bud were already down the road.

CHAPTER 7
HORSE WIVES

Bristol was angry with everyone. Nancy and Elise had their nerve to lecture her! Why was everyone so stupid? Lavern was just a wimp who couldn't face her husband. Jolene was a dumb kid who didn't think her mother would see through her conniving to meet with that boyfriend of hers who thought he was already a veterinarian. And Bud!

Bud had followed her part way home. At the intersection where he would turn toward his home, she pulled over so they could stop to talk. She invited him to sit in her truck with her, but he stood outside of her open window. He wouldn't make any plans with her. She tried to set up a campout date with him and a Friday night at the Amped Up, but he would not commit to anything. He walked away to his own rig without even telling her that he would call her later, and so far he hadn't. Of course, it was only Monday morning.

Maybe the person she was most angry with was her husband, Ric. When she came home yesterday afternoon, Ric was not there. Something about the house seemed empty. She walked through it feeling a cold chill. In the entrance hallway, his jacket was not on the hook. In the living room, many of the CDs were gone. In the bedroom, the change jar on top of his dresser was missing. She opened the closet and his clothes were gone. She opened his dresser drawers and none of his clothes were there.

Ric had not left a note. There were no voice mail messages from him on the answering machine. There were only several calls from Charlie trying to find Lavern and asking for a return call.

Tears stung the backs of her eyes, but she jammed her fists into them, determined not to cry. Ric was not worth it! He would either come crawling back when he discovered how little she would leave him in a divorce, or Bud would call again, or she would meet someone else. She refused to think about how she would handle caring for this property and for her horse if Ric did not come home. Already she had to set her alarm earlier this morning so she could feed Hot Stuff herself. Tonight she would have to clean his stall and fill the water tub if Ric wasn't home. He better be home by the weekend because the pasture and the yard would need to be mowed!

She had just arrived at work with all of these angry thoughts swirling in her head. She was a few minutes late because of the extra time it took her this morning at home. She walked into the office where the staff greeted her with silence. Yes, she was angry with them, too. They were never friendly. They refused to come to the Amped Up to hear her sing, and they talked about her behind her back, she was pretty sure.

Before she could reach her own office, her boss, Larry Brown, came down the hallway toward her. "Bristol, I need to see you. Please come to my office."

"Sure, Larry, be right there," she answered, puzzled. She dumped her purse in her desk drawer and walked down the hall to find Mr. Stokes in the office with Larry. Mr. Stokes was the big boss from the home office. Bristol was surprised to see him. Maybe they were going to give her a promotion or something.

She held out her hand to him. "Hello, Mr. Stokes. It's nice to see you."

Stokes did not take her hand. "Bristol, we have a problem." He remained standing, stiff in his pinstripe suit and tie. He did not invite Bristol to sit down. Larry sat behind his desk, frowning.

"It has come to our attention that you have not been operating this office in an above-board manner. We have had some complaints from the office staff here, several in fact, and we feel that it is time to part company with you."

"What?" Bristol was shocked. She sank into the visitor's chair and tried to gather her wits. This was the last thing she would have ever expected. "What do you mean? I don't have any written reprimands. You can't fire me. I do good work. Ask Larry. What's going on? Who set me up?"

"I *have* discussed this with Mr. Brown, extensively, in fact. I have also been discussing this with our legal department. After receiving complaints, we have been watching you more closely. Mr. Brown has agreed that the allegations appear to be legitimate. Legal feels that we can end this quickly by offering you an early retirement compensation. Or, if you prefer to stay, we can write up every complaint and discuss each one with you, creating the necessary documentation for a legal dismissal, and, of course, adding any future complaints, discussions, and reprimands to your personnel record. I'm convinced that there would be additional complaints."

Bristol started to speak, but no words came to mind. She looked at Larry, hoping that he would back her up, but Larry backed up Stokes. "Bristol, you have two weeks of vacation due. I suggest that you take it, beginning today. We can mail you an agreement for your early retirement compensation. Sign it and send it back. Think how much more time this will give you for enjoying your horse."

Bristol's face was red, and her mouth moved like a fish. Finally, she realized that if she did not agree to the early retirement, she would be fired and would receive no compensation. "How much are you offering me?" she asked.

It was a very small amount, plus the two-week paid vacation, but it was better than nothing, and she did not want to go through the embarrassment of the disciplinary process. She guessed that probably most of the complaints were valid, but she was surprised that the women in the office reported her.

She stalked out of Larry's office, grabbed her set of office keys from her own office, and stalked back down the hall where she threw the keys at Mr. Stokes, hitting him in his chest. Pleased with the accuracy of her aim, she would have laughed if she had not been so upset.

Back in her own office, she grabbed the two photos of Hot Stuff from her desk, and her purse from the drawer, and left. After driving around aimlessly for an hour, fuming, she went home. There really was nowhere else to go. She needed to cool off and think.

In the house she noticed the red blinking light telling her there was new voice mail. She played it. There was nothing from Ric or Bud. There were two more messages from Charlie. She called him back.

"Hey, Charlie, this is Bristol. I know where Lavern is. She's at the horseman's camp in Harrison State Forest in Cadiz, Ohio."

****

Elise had a heart-to-heart talk with Jolene on their drive home from Harrison. Elise had explained that she was disappointed in her daughter for being manipulative about having Randy join them on the campout. It led to a worthwhile discussion about the value of good character. That led to a discussion that focused on Bristol's lack of character and how it affected her reputation.

"Don't worry, Mom. I would never use Bristol as a role model except as how *not* to be." Then Jolene actually apologized to her mother. "Mom, I'm sorry. I know I wasn't upfront with you, but I knew that you would say no if I asked if Randy could come with us. I know that's no excuse to have done it, but it's the reason I did it. I really like Randy. I want to spend as much time as I can with him this summer. I think he might go to Ohio State this fall. He applied there for a scholarship. If it comes through, he'll transfer there, and I won't be able to see him much anymore."

"Honey, your apology is accepted. I really should punish you and forbid you to see him for the next two weeks, but I'm not going to."

Jolene gave a relieved sigh.

"I did something like that when I was sixteen," Elise went on.

"What did you do?" Jolene was curious.

"Well, I really shouldn't tell you."

"Oh, come on, Mom. You can't tell me that much and then not tell me the rest."

"Well, my boyfriend wanted to make out with me, and we never had anywhere to go to do that. He talked me into letting him into the house after my parents went to bed. He said he would be at our back door at midnight, and that I should let him in. I was scared silly of being caught, but I did it. We tried making out on the couch, but I was so nervous that I couldn't stop shaking. When I say shaking, I mean really shaking hard. I thought sure that we would wake up my parents, and they would be so disappointed in me. Finally he got mad at me and left. I was never so glad to see him go!"

"You were sixteen? Oh, Mom!"

That led to a conversation about making out and premarital sex. Jolene assured her mother that she was still a virgin and intended to stay that way until she was married. "If I get married before I'm seventeen, anyway," she added.

"What! Young lady!"

"Mom, I'm joking. Don't worry. I do take intimacy seriously."

Their discussion helped them rediscover a closeness that had been missing for awhile, and Elise felt a little better about Jolene dating Randy, although she was still concerned. She hoped that Randy's scholarship would come through and that he would leave for Ohio State in Columbus in the fall. She did not have long to wait for her answer.

Randy called on Monday asking to visit. When he came over, he told Elise and Jolene about receiving the scholarship. He was happy, and Jolene tried to act happy for him, but Elise could tell that she was disappointed.

Elise watched them walk hand in hand to the barn. She tried hard to hold onto the trust she placed in Jolene. She also hoped that Jolene was not crushed knowing that Randy would soon be leaving for school.

Elise was baking Jolene's favorite cookies when Jolene returned to the house alone. Elise expected her to go to her room to brood, but Jolene flopped on the settee in the sunroom. Elise took the first batch of cookies from the oven, placed several on a plate, and took them into the sunroom on a tray with two glasses of lemonade. She sat down next to her daughter.

Jolene smiled sadly and took a cookie. "Thanks, Mom."

"Are you OK?"

"Yeah, sure," she answered, only partially convincing. "You know, there's another good thing about not sleeping with a guy. If he goes out of town and can't date you for a long time, you can date others without feeling like you're doing anything wrong. Unless, of course, you have promised each other not to date anyone else, but who would be dumb enough to do that? I mean, I wouldn't want to miss my junior prom or homecoming or anything because he was stuck in Columbus."

Elise just listened to her ramble.

"I mean, like, I don't like the idea of Randy dating anyone else, but I guess he will. I know he likes me. I sure like him. Maybe if he dates others, he'll compare them to me, and he would like me even more. I guess the summer will tell us a lot. He wants to take me out Saturday night. Can we go riding with him again next week?"

Jolene's face crumpled into tears, and Elise moved over to hold her daughter and stroke her long blond hair. Elise was happy that Jolene was confiding in her. Elise was happy with her daughter's view of the situation. Elise was happy with this new closeness. Elise was happy.

****

Monday afternoon, Nancy, Lavern, Bree, and Cadey returned from their ride. They had done trail maintenance on the red trail for two hours and had ridden to the end of the green trail. They had eaten their lunch and then had ridden back to camp via the blue and yellow trails. They were now each in their own campsites tending their horses.

They unsaddled, washed down their horses with water, and tied them onto their picket lines. If they had not hung a fresh bale of hay before the ride, they had to do so now. No horse was given a drink of water until it had cooled off.

Lavern walked down the hill to the restroom in the middle of the horseman's camp. She was just finishing when she heard two shots fired, hitting the fiberglass roof. Startled and scared, several thoughts came to her in a split second. She wondered how Charlie had found her, she did not want him to trap her inside the restroom, and she worried that not only was he going to shoot her, but he would also shoot Lacy. She zipped up her jeans while running out of the building, looking around wildly, hoping to save Lacy without being shot herself.

Bree and Cadey were sitting in their lawn chairs by the fire ring, laughing at her.

"That old horse chestnut tree got you!" Bree told her. It sometimes drops those green chestnuts onto the restroom roof. It sounded like shots, didn't it?"

"Yes, they got her," Cadey said. "Come on, join us over here. We're going to plan our supper. We thought we would eat together again tonight. Do you and Nancy want to join us?"

"Yeah, sure. I have plenty of food, so I could bring something for both Nancy and myself. I don't know what she has since she wasn't really planning to stay this long. Here she comes."

Lavern sat in her chair that was already at the fire ring. She was still a little shaky from the adrenaline rush. Nancy, carrying her folding chair, joined the group. Bree stacked logs and started a fire. Cadey left to fill the coffee pot with water and throw in a half a cup of coffee grounds to make some cowboy coffee over the fire.

When Nancy had settled in her chair, she told Lavern, "I just talked to my sister. She asked if she and Harry could turn my sewing room into a bedroom for her to stay right in the house with us. I'm so happy! She was going to apartment hunt, but it will save her money to just stay with us, and she'll be there more often to help with Mom."

"Cool! What needs to be done to the room?" Lavern asked.

"Not much. My sewing machine and materials need to be taken to the basement, and the closet needs to be cleared out for her clothes. My off-season clothes are in there now. I guess they have to go into the basement. I told her if they want to paint in there to go ahead."

Bree looked up from where she crouched over the fire pit. "Will your clothes be OK in the basement?"

"Oh, yeah. Our basement is dry. They should be OK. Actually, I'll probably go through all of my clothes and get rid of what I don't wear anymore, and everything will fit in my bedroom closet then."

"So, Lavern!" Nancy turned to her. "We don't know how long Sis will live with us, but while she does, she will need to store her furniture. She could pay for storage, or..." Nancy paused, "she could loan it to you to use until you want to buy some of your own.

Would that help you out?"

Lavern grinned. "Oh, yes, it really would be a help. It would give me time to save up some money. Thank you for thinking of me."

"No problem. The only thing Sis will need at my house is her bed, but you know what? You can have one of Mom's beds from her house. She doesn't need any of them anymore."

They made plans for taking the furniture to Lavern's new apartment. By the time that was settled, the coffee was ready. Bree poured everyone a cup and they sat around the fire making dinner plans. When Bree and Cadey left for their trailers to start cooking, Nancy asked Lavern how she was doing.

"Oh, I'm fine. Don't worry about me. I feel so much contentment now that I don't have to worry about Charlie and what could make him angry. I'm going to enjoy this summer, then I'm going to enjoy my new apartment and teaching a new class of kids again."

The sound of a motorcycle on the road leading into camp startled Lavern.

"I'm fine, except for the times I think Charlie might be around, that is. It really scared me when those buckeye things fell on the restroom roof. I thought he was out there shooting. And now I hear a motorcycle, and it makes me worry that he's coming."

The sound of the motorcycle grew louder. They both looked down the camp road. It was Charlie on his red Honda roaring into camp. They both stood.

Nancy told her, "Run and hide, Lavern. Quick!"

"I can't. He'll hurt Lacy. I'll just have to face him."

Nancy stood protectively in front of Lavern as Charlie left his bike on the camp road and stomped toward them, an outraged grimace on his angry red face.

"What the hell do you think you're doing, woman?" he shouted at Lavern. He started around Nancy to grab Lavern's arm. Lavern backed up, and Nancy sidestepped in front of Charlie, blocking his way. "Get over here and get on that bike. We're going home!" he yelled at Lavern.

Lavern's voice was soft and controlled even though she was quaking inside. "No, Charlie, it's over between us. I'm staying here. You go on and get out of here."

Charlie again tried to step around Nancy, but she again sidestepped to remain in between Lavern and Charlie. Charlie gave an outraged cry and grabbed Nancy's shoulders and threw her to the ground. Nancy cried out in shock and pain. Lavern backed up three steps before Charlie caught her.

He smacked Lavern's face. "I said, you're coming home with me where you belong. Don't sass me, and don't mock me." He smacked her face again.

Lavern backed up again, and Charlie leapt at her and grabbed her hair. He pulled hard and had Lavern standing on her tip toes. With his other hand, he punched her in her ribs. The air whooshed out of her, and she doubled over. He punched her ribs twice more. He let go of her hair and grabbed her arm, twirling her around, her back now to his chest.

"Walk!" he ordered as he tried to push her forward.

"No," she cried. "I'm staying here." She tried to fall to the ground to escape his grip, but he held her up.

"I told you not to sass me." Now Charlie's voice was low and dangerous. With one arm he held Lavern tight to his chest, her hands uselessly imprisoned between them, and he put his other arm around her neck and began squeezing. She tried to kick him with her feet, but he only squeezed tighter. Her face was turning a red-purple. She struggled harder, trying to free herself from his grip.

Suddenly Charlie screamed. Cadey had come up behind him and jabbed him in his back with a pitchfork deep enough to draw blood. Bree had grabbed the coffee pot off the fire and poured what was left of the boiling liquid down his back. Charlie dropped Lavern who now lay gasping on the ground. He started for Bree and Cadey, but Cadey held the pitchfork in front of them, ready to strike Charlie again.

"Stop! Stop! Everyone stop! Hold it right there! Nobody move!" It was the forest ranger running into the camp circle. He had come into the camp to check on things and talk with the campers, never expecting to find trouble.

Nancy was sitting on the ground holding her head. Lavern was on her knees on the ground. Her lip was split and her eye was already swelling shut. Her neck was red where Charlie had been squeezing. She was gasping for breath. Bree had dropped the coffee pot at her feet and Cadey was still pointing the pitchfork at Charlie.

Charlie was still enraged. He turned and kicked Lavern in her already-sore ribs. She screamed in pain. Charlie reached down to pull her to her feet, but the ranger grabbed Charlie by the back of his blood soaked shirt. Charlie yelled and turned to swing at the ranger. The ranger ducked the blow, but before he was able to handcuff him, Charlie connected solidly with the ranger's nose causing a spray of blood. "Son, you're in a heap of trouble now." The ranger cuffed him and wiped the blood from his face.

"No, not me. These women attacked me! Look, it was four against one. Check my back! Can't a man defend himself?"

"Sorry, Son, but I saw enough of what was happening that you're going to jail. Get going. I'm putting you in the back of my car." The ranger steered Charlie to the car and pushed him inside. He called the local sheriff department and asked for an ambulance for Lavern and a deputy to take Charlie to booking.

"What about me? They burned me and they stabbed me. I need a doctor."

"Yes, Son, I suppose you do. I'm sure the deputy sheriff will see that you receive medical attention. Now, shut up."

While waiting for the deputy, the ranger took detailed reports from each of the women.

When he had the full story, he told Lavern that at least for now, she would not have to worry about Charlie. He was sure to receive a long jail sentence for his attack on her, Nancy, and the ranger himself. "It was attempted murder on you, Missy," he told Lavern. "I'm glad I was here, but truth to tell, your friends had it pretty well handled."

The ambulance arrived from Cadiz. The paramedics checked the Ranger's nose, and then they transported Lavern to the hospital. The hospital staff x-rayed Lavern's ribs and stitched her lip. They told her that her ribs were bruised, not broken. They recommended ice for her eye and her neck and gave her a prescription for pain pills. They photographed her injuries for forensic evidence. Bree picked her up from the emergency room, took her to a pharmacy, and brought her back to camp.

The ranger stopped by again as the women sat around the fire finishing their late dinner. He assured the group that Charlie was indeed in jail, and that he expected him to be there for a long time. "Of course, you will each have to testify if it goes to trial, but I expect him to take a plea bargain. They charged him with felonious assault on Lavern and on me. Assaulting a peace officer is a first degree felony and can bring eleven years in prison. Assaulting Lavern was a second degree felony which could get him eight years. Assaulting Nancy was a misdemeanor, even though she did not sustain a provable injury. That would give him up to six months in jail. I was hoping for attempted murder on Lavern, but even with a plea bargain to minimize his time, he should be gone for several years."

All of the women, and especially Lavern, were grateful that the ranger had come by to let them know. They would be sleeping easier tonight with Charlie in jail.

****

Three months later, Charlie was on his way to prison. Lavern, now divorced from Charlie, was settled in her new apartment with furniture borrowed from Nancy's sister, and she was enjoying teaching her new class of students.

Nancy was less stressed because her sister, who had quickly found a nursing job in the local hospital, was living in her home and helping to care for their mother.

Elise was enjoying a better relationship with her daughter. Jolene was writing letters to Randy while dating a boy of her own age from her high school who was going to take her to the homecoming dance.

Bristol was job hunting, and she was fighting a divorce trying to keep most of the assets from the marriage. Bud did not return her calls. They all rode their horses every weekend. Bristol rode alone.   And   so   it   goes…

Questions for Discussion

1) Do you ever pray for people you do not like?

2) Can you forgive people who are still causing you problems?

3) Do you agree that there is some good even in the most unlikeable person?

4) What do you do to keep the lines of communication open with your children and other family members?

5) Is there someone in your life that you need to forgive?

6) Who do you need to pray for today?

ABOUT THE AUTHOR

Janet earned her B.A. in Education from the University of Akron in Ohio. She has had a love of horses her whole life. She lives on a five acre horse farm with the love of her life, Jack, their border collie, Bailey, and their Tennessee Walker horses that they take horse camping and trail riding. Janet enjoys making scrapbooks with the photos she takes while riding. She encourages all riders to wear a helmet. She can be reached at:

JanetRFox_Author@mail.com

On Face Book as Janet R Fox Author

Made in the USA
Charleston, SC
16 February 2016